CW00647517

BULLFIGHT

YASUSHI INOUE

BULLFIGHT

Translated by
Michael Emmerich

PUSHKIN PRESS
LONDON

Pushkin Press
71–75 Shelton Street, London WC2H 9JQ

Bullfight was originally published as 闘牛 (*Tōgyū*).
This translation is based on the text in *Inoue Yasushi zenshū*
(*Collected Works of Yasushi Inoue*), Tokyo, Shinchōsha (1995–1997).

This translation first published by Pushkin Press in 2013

ISBN 978 1 782270 00 3

Frontispiece: *Yasushi Inoue*, reproduced with
permission of The Wylie Agency

Set in 10.5 on 15 Monotype Baskerville
by Tetragon, London

Proudly printed and bound in Great Britain
by TJ International, Padstow, Cornwall
on Munken Premium White 90gsm

www.pushkinpress.com

BULLFIGHT

THE LARGE, eye-catching announcement ran in the *Osaka New Evening Post* in mid-December 1946: early the next year, from January 20, the paper would sponsor a three-day bullfighting tournament at Hanshin Baseball Stadium. As soon as the page proofs came off the presses, Tsugami, the editor-in-chief, slipped a copy into his pocket, collected Tashiro, whom he had left to his own devices in the chilly reception room long enough already, and stepped out with him into what one might describe as a classically wintry afternoon—air that over the past two or three days had become genuinely cold, gusts of biting wind that kept starting restlessly up off the street.

"Ah, it's out!" Tashiro took the newspaper Tsugami offered him and peered intently down at it, his expression relaxing into a brief, uncharacteristic smile, only to turn serious again an instant later. "From here on you just have to keep advertising, right up to the very end..." The paper flapped in the wind as he strode forward; he folded the few sheets in four and shoved them in his pocket. "Speaking of which, there's something else I'd like to talk to you about, if you don't mind."

Tashiro never seemed to tire. By the time he had one project on track, he was already heading toward his next goal. They had expended an enormous amount of energy just getting to the stage where they could finally print this notice, but none of that seemed to have had any effect on him.

"So how's this for a plan—why not buy the bulls? All twenty-two. Say they're fifty thousand yen a head, that comes to a million one hundred thousand. A bargain, right? It'd be really easy if the paper bought them, and my guess is the people down in W., at the Association, as long as you're interested they'll be willing."

Tashiro rattled on without a pause, so focused you would have thought he had come all the way up from Kyushu specifically to make this proposal. The paper could sell the twenty-two bulls right away, as soon as the tournament was over, without having to go to the bother of looking after them. Of course, if they could afford to let their investment rest a while, they could hold on to them, see how the situation developed. After going to all the trouble of hauling twenty-two bulls up from Shikoku, though, all that distance, they couldn't just send the animals back the second the tournament ended, right? You got more guts than that! Buy the bulls for a million one hundred thousand, right, and just transporting them to the Hanshin area ought to make it possible to turn that into a million and five or six hundred thousand. And if you could put them to sleep and turn them into meat, well, that would be a bit of a hassle, but right there you're talking two million yen easy. Such, at any rate, were Tashiro's calculations.

A thick-set and broad-shouldered man of average height, Tashiro was bundled from head to toe in a heavy leather overcoat; he carried a somewhat aged but still stiff alligator-skin Boston bag—the sort of thing that had become rather valuable of late. Every so often as they hurried along the largely deserted, bombed-out street toward Midōsuji he would stop in his tracks, anxious that the wind hitting their faces was preventing Tsugami from hearing him, and stand there with his head lifted, talking to his taller companion.

Tsugami listened, nodding, though obviously he had no intention of getting involved in any such scheme. The *Osaka New Evening Post* had been established with a hundred and ninety-five thousand yen; given how small it was, it was no exaggeration to say that sponsoring the tournament was already more than it could manage. This was a gamble on whose success the future of the company depended. Their finances were so strained right now that they had struggled just to scrape together funding for the tournament itself; the idea of buying the bulls was so ambitious as to be ludicrous. The paper had gotten started a year ago, in December 1945, with a staff composed largely of former employees of *B. News*, known as one of the two biggest newspapers in the country; even after all these months, they still relied on the larger paper for everything from typesetting and printing to photographs and use of its liaison department. People tended to assume as a result that *Osaka New Evening Post* was a subsidiary of *B. News*, and was run using the same capital. In actual fact, despite all appearances to the contrary, there was no connection at all between the two papers' management. Tashiro, who was as sly a showman as any you were likely to find, had surely made a thorough investigation of the *Osaka New Evening Post*'s finances before contracting to help out with the tournament; that he was proposing such a substantial investment even so, suggested that he had overestimated the significance of the connection with *B. News*, and assumed that any losses would be covered, even if things went awry. For him to make so grand a misjudgment concerning a little paper that had only been around for a year—to be trying so earnestly to interest its editor in a *second* big project on top of the tournament—revealed a naïve optimism that seemed utterly typical of a country showman, and at the same time a willingness to drop all pretenses once you had started working together, to expose his true nature as a schemer, that was so open and unabashed it made you want to avert your eyes.

Still, Tsugami felt no particular misgivings or anxiety about collaborating with Tashiro on this event. He had, he thought, made a fairly accurate assessment of his character as a showman when they first met—his cunning, his shamelessness, the likelihood that he would stray from the straight and narrow if it proved necessary to bring in a bit of money. He had no fear, despite all of this, that he would get burned in the course of their collaboration. In part this was because he sensed that there was a limit to how deep these admittedly caution-inspiring traits went—test any one of them and you would hit bottom soon enough—but more reassuring still was the oddly pure enthusiasm Tashiro showed for his work on occasion, a sort of passion that made Tsugami think with a start that he himself probably had a lot more bad inside him than Tashiro. "I'm telling you, this is going to be huge!" he would say, stressing each word, rolling each one around in his mouth, his expression radiating an incongruent air of abstraction. His gaze, at such moments, would be fixed in midair, as if he were watching something in the distance, and as the seconds passed he would slowly turn his eyes upward, higher and higher. It was as though some mysterious flower only Tashiro could see was hovering there, airborne, calling to him from afar. His mind, then, was free of calculations. Tsugami would regard with an unforgiving eye the stupid expression of this showman who had let all thought of profits and losses slip from his mind, his attitude that of a man examining a sculpture, and then all of a sudden he would find himself looking coldly into his own heart, which was no longer capable of losing itself in anything.

"And if the paper doesn't buy them?" Tsugami asked.

"Actually," Tashiro said, his tone suggesting that he had been waiting for Tsugami to ask precisely this question, "someone else has said he'd like to buy them. Matter of fact, that's why I've imposed upon you today like this—I'd like you to come meet him. I wanted to have someone lined up, you see, just in case the paper isn't interested. You could make it a joint investment, if you like, and even apart from this, I'm sure he can be of assistance in other ways. His name is Okabe Yata—perhaps you've heard of him? He's quite a man, I must say."

Coming from Tashiro, that "quite a man" didn't bode well. But Tsugami decided that if Tashiro wanted him to go meet this man, he would do him that favor—today, at any rate, he could do that. The relief he felt now that they had made it this far, now that the notice was about to go in the paper, had left him feeling buoyant and willing to oblige.

"He's from my hometown. I really look up to him, though he's a bit younger than me. He's one impressive guy, really. President of Hanshin Industries, though he owns three or four other companies, too. No one else from Iyo has made it as big as him."

No sooner had Tashiro said his piece than he leaned his broad, screen-like body forward and started walking on again, striding forward with big steps.

*

Tashiro Sutematsu had first presented himself at Tsugami's house in Nishinomiya about a month ago, proffering an extra-large business card that described him rather dubiously as "President of Umewaka Entertainment." As a rule Tsugami never received work visitors at home, but Sakiko had come over the previous evening and they had started quarreling, as they always did, about whether or not to break up; this morning, Tsugami was more than happy to have an excuse to escape the icy glitter in her eyes, the stubborn silence that could be read as expressing either love or hatred.

Tsugami's first meeting with Tashiro left him with the impression that he was precisely what his business card said he was: a country showman. His lively, ruddy face and his booming voice gave him a relatively young air, but he was clearly well past fifty. His double-breasted, brown homespun jacket and his wide-striped shirt were flashy enough for a man in his twenties, and he wore two silver rings on his coarse, stubby fingers; oddly, even after he came inside he kept his thin black muffler, which was the only part of his outfit that looked cheap, wrapped around his neck.

Tashiro was trying to sell a bullfighting tournament. After outlining the origins and the history of "bull sumo," which existed only in the town of W., in Iyo, and nowhere else in Japan, he went on to explain in a cadence that verged at times on the incantatory, as though he were addressing an audience, that the one thing he most wanted in life was to be able to introduce this traditional local sport to the rest of the country.

"I myself, it is true, am just a nameless showman, no different from any other, but bullfighting is special—my efforts to promote it are unrelated to my business. I'm fortunate enough to have various other sources of income. As a matter of fact, you could say I've been touring the island of Shikoku with local theater troupes and naniwa-bushi performers these past thirty years, none of the troupes particularly good, solely on account of this dream I've cherished that one day I would have a chance to take Iyo bull sumo up to Tokyo or Osaka, to bring the sport into the limelight."

Despite his protestation that this was not a business venture, Tashiro emphasized more than once that it would be very hard indeed to find a project more certain to yield a profit.

Tsugami sat with his pipe in his mouth, allowing himself to be swept up in the overdramatic flood of words Tashiro directed at him; he gazed out at the trunk of the sasanqua in the corner of the small garden, his eyes cold and unmoved. He met with characters like this every day at work. His practice was to listen noncommittally with half of his mind, while he allowed the other half to lose itself in utterly unrelated, often deeply lonely musings. From the speaker's perspective it was like sticking a lance into something again and again with no result, although when Tsugami did offer the odd brief comment it would be so precisely attuned to the moment, for all its rote conversationality, that the visitor would succumb to the peculiar illusion that Tsugami was actually listening in rapt attention.

Tsugami grew ever more impassive; Tashiro waxed increasingly eloquent.

"Now, when someone mentions bullfighting, people who don't know much about it will assume it must be a very rowdy, boorish sport, but I assure you this could not be further from the truth. The thing is, you see, from time immemorial the locals have always bet on which of the—"

"They bet?" Tsugami exclaimed.

According to Tashiro, tournaments were held three times each year in W., and even now almost everyone who attended gambled on the matches. Until then Tashiro's words had passed Tsugami by without having any effect, but somehow, in an odd and warped way, this bit of information managed to penetrate his mind. All at once, in the most natural manner, Tashiro had caused the scene to rise up before Tsugami like a frame from a movie: the vast modern bleachers at Hanshin Stadium or Kōroen Stadium; the contest between two living creatures playing itself out within a bamboo enclosure at the center; the riveted spectators; the loudspeakers; the bundles of bills; the rocking, cheering waves of people... It was a slow-moving, cold, but distinctly palpable picture, executed in lead. After that, Tsugami hardly paid any attention to what Tashiro was saying. Betting, he was thinking, yes, this could work. Everyone would put money on the bulls—it would be no different here in the urban Hanshin region than it was in W. In these postwar days, perhaps this was just the sort of thing the Japanese needed if they were going to keep struggling through their lives. Set up some random event for people to bet on, and everything would take care of itself: they would come and place their bets. Just imagine it—tens of thousands of spectators betting on a bullfight in a stadium hemmed in on every side by the ruined city. It could work. Baseball and rugby were finally getting started again, but it would be two or three years still until they could regain their former popularity. In times like these, bull sumo was as much as people could manage. The first bullfighting tournament in Hanshin, ever—not a bad project for a newspaper to sponsor, not bad at all. In the short term, at least, the *Osaka New Evening Post* was unlikely to find anything better.

Tsugami's eyes, as he sat thinking these thoughts, had the same moist, untamed look in them, cold and yet somehow viscous, burning, that made it impossible for Sakiko to leave him, try as she might. He sat up and said, in a sharp, conclusive tone completely different from the one he had used before, "I'll think it over. You know, this might just be the thing."

Half an hour or so later Tashiro left, and in the sudden stillness of the room Tsugami realized that he was mildly excited. As was his habit when he began planning a new project, he sat for a long time in a chair out on the verandah, saying little and moving not at all. At such times, he wanted more than anything to be alone.

Suddenly, Sakiko's voice broke the silence. "You'd love a project like that."

She was sitting in a corner of the room in the same posture she had been in before Tsugami went outside, her head down, knitting needles glinting white and cold in her hands.

"Why do you say that?"

"Oh, I don't know, just seems that way. You'd get totally wrapped up in it, I can tell. You've got that side to you." Then, raising her eyes and casting a quick, cold glance his way, she said in a tone that could have been either reproachful or resigned, "The unsavory side."

She was right. The word described a certain facet of his personality.

Tsugami had been one of the best reporters in the city news section at *B. News*, and as such he had made his way largely unscathed through three years as deputy managing editor of that ever troublesome section—a job at which everyone else had failed. The creases in his pants were invariably crisp; he was nimble both in his interactions with visitors and in the manner in which he disposed of his work, and sharp to the extent that he sometimes came across as unfeeling. No matter how odious the incident, he could always find some clever way to soften it in print. Naturally, he had made his share of enemies in a world populated by demanding journalists. They said he was loose with money, or smug, or an egoist, or a stylist, or a literature boy, and to an extent the criticisms they leveled at him hit the mark; but these very faults lent him an intellectual air that set him apart from most city news reporters.

When the war ended, *B. News* decided that the most rational way of dealing with its huge surplus staff was to establish a printing company and an evening newspaper; it moved a significant number of employees to these affiliated companies. Tsugami was immediately tapped to become the new paper's editor-in-chief. At thirty-seven he seemed slightly young for the post, but clearly no one else had the abundant talent required to create a brand-new kind of publication capable of beating the competition at a time when countless such papers kept sprouting up; and since Omoto, the former film-industry man who had landed in the president's seat, was a total amateur who didn't know the first thing about producing a newspaper, whose only selling point was his boldness, what they needed above all was a solid, reliable individual capable not only of working under the president, taking charge of the editing, but also of serving as the central axle around which the paper's management would revolve. In this respect, too, the impression of thoroughness and caution that Tsugami had given his colleagues had played strongly to his advantage.

When Tsugami assumed his position as editor-in-chief of the *Osaka New Evening Post*, he first made the bold decision to give the paper a new format, wider than it was long; then, having clearly identified its target readership as urban intellectuals and salarymen, he settled on culture and entertainment as the two subjects for which it would be known, and decided to emphasize satire, irony, and wit in every aspect of its reportage, from its prose style to its coverage and editing. This innovative path he chose for the *New Evening Post* achieved a certain measure of success: it gained popularity as a different breed of publication among salarymen, students, and the like throughout the entire region, in Kyoto, Osaka, and Kobe, and when the street hawkers came around it was the first to sell out. A paper of this sort had a genuinely attractive freshness in the eyes of readers accustomed to the oafish wartime papers. A certain young professor at Kyoto University, who had been restored to his post after the war ended, commented in a mini column he wrote for the university newspaper that the *New Evening Post* was "a paper for the slightly unsavory intellectual," and to an extent he was right. A sensitive poet type would undoubtedly have been able to point out a certain shadow of emptiness, of devil-may-care negligence, of loneliness darkening the pages of a paper that was popular among smart city kids. These were qualities that Tsugami, who gave the paper its editorial direction, carried within himself, though he kept them carefully concealed. The one person who had sniffed out these elements of his personality better than anyone was Sakiko, the woman with whom he had been living off and on for three years now, since the middle of the war, and who kept insisting she was going to leave him, this time she really was, only to let their hopeless relationship keep dragging on and on.

"No one else knows you have this side to you," she would say when she was feeling happy. "This sneaky, sloppy, unsavory side. No one else, just me."

Her eyes would shine, as though that element of Tsugami's character were a trace of the love she had given him. On other occasions, however, she would utter the exact same words but as a criticism directed at her lover.

Tsugami had a wife and two children who were still living in his hometown in Tottori, where he had sent them to escape the bombing; Sakiko had a husband, a college friend of Tsugami's, who had died at war and whose bones had not yet come home. Tsugami and Sakiko had first gotten involved while the war was still on, and their relationship continued just as it was after the fighting ended. Still, even Tsugami's colleagues at the newspaper, who usually had such sharp eyes when it came to things like this, had yet to catch wind of their affair—a circumstance that Sakiko interpreted, at least at times, as another sign of his cunning.

Sakiko had first become physically involved with Tsugami about a year after she was notified, by back channels, of her husband's death. She had been in the habit of going and talking with Tsugami whenever she wanted to discuss her plans for the future, and one summer evening she had gone to visit him at home. He had only just come back from the office, and when she walked around to the verandah as she usually did she found him slumped in a wicker chair inside the house, still dressed in his work clothes, his hat tipped back on his head, taking sips from a glass of whiskey with the attitude of a man who just doesn't care anymore.

The second he noticed Sakiko, Tsugami leaped up and straightened his jacket, transforming himself into his usual proper, austere self, but by then Sakiko could already feel the blood stirring hotly in her body—a sensation she had all but forgotten. There had been something forlorn in the sight of him there, unguarded, exhausted, that left her oddly moved, touched in a sensuous, moist way. Even after they started sleeping together, she still remembered Tsugami the way she had seen him that evening, and felt that the man she had encountered then was who she loved, that isolated, lonely soul no one else knew, that was somehow being eaten away, emitting a sort of rotten phosphorescence.

Tsugami's love was not the sort that burned hot and deep. Somewhere down inside him was a core that refused to catch. She could throw herself bodily into his arms and still she would sense that same unbridgeable gap between them. Tsugami's eyes were unassailably sober, untouched by Sakiko's heart or by her thirty-year-old body. His were not a lover's eyes. But neither were they the eyes of a man who would simply toss her aside, like a piece of trash on the road. He gazed at her like an outside observer, watching from a distance, waiting to see how matters would develop—cold, fish-like, and therefore irresistible.

Whenever Sakiko brushed up against this coldness in Tsugami's heart, so deep he himself seemed unsure how to handle it, the same phrase rose up in her mind: *a bad man*. But there were times when those emotionless, wicked eyes of his would push themselves toward drunkenness. Sakiko knew that very well. How she loved Tsugami for those eyes: their frenzied, lawless, mournful light. But then she realized that she would never be able to strip them of their sobriety, and her love began, from time to time, to turn itself into a hatred that glistened with sadness.

The fact that Tsugami had let himself be tugged along so easily by the bait Tashiro offered him, by the thought of the bullfight, may perhaps have owed less to his reporter's instincts than to those sober eyes of his, and the rebellious urge he felt to make them drunk, finally, for once, on something. Sakiko had been right to speak of the hidden "unsavory side" of his personality.

*

The day after Tashiro came to talk about the bullfight, Tashiro convened a meeting in the remodeled building where the *Osaka New Evening Post* had its offices—a structure in Yatsuhashi that had survived the firebombings. Also in attendance were Omoto, the paper's president; K., director of the copyediting department; S., advertising director; and Tashiro.

Omoto immediately gave the project his approval. "Terrific idea, I love it. We'll have to sponsor it ourselves, with support from the town of W. and the Bull Sumo Association—that's the way to do it. We ought to be able to bring in a hundred and fifty thousand people over three days, I'd say, assuming fifty thousand a day. We'll go big on publicity, like we brought the bulls over from Spain or something."

Omoto was so corpulent he looked like a somewhat poorly trained fighting bull himself, and was talking so loudly he was almost shouting, as was his wont when his mood was good. Having raised himself by his own bootstraps from a humble beginning as the owner of a movie theater out in the country to his present position, he had confidence and guts when it came to business matters; he was the sort of man who decided everything on the basis of his own inimitable instincts. Now that Omoto and Tsugami were in favor of the bullfight, no one else could possibly express any real opposition. And so, just like that, the issue was decided. They would bring the tournament that was held at S. Shrine in W. each New Year's Day up here and hold it in one or the other of the two gigantic, modern baseball stadiums in the Hanshin area. They would have to work on the town and the Bull Sumo Association to make sure to get their support, both in name and in terms of the actual logistics. The tournament would be held over the course of three days in late January, during the off season for outdoor sports. The newspaper and Umewaka Entertainment would split the difference between total expenditure and total income—they would share all profits or losses, in other words. Umewaka Entertainment would not be mentioned in any of the publicity, however; as far as the public knew, the tournament would be carried out solely under the auspices of the *Osaka New Evening Post.* The expenses that accumulated along the way, until they did their final calculation at the conclusion of the tournament, would be divided with Tashiro taking responsibility for the costs of renting the bulls and transporting them to the stadium while the paper covered whatever costs there were after their arrival, along with those of readying the stadium, doing other preparatory work, and advertising the event. Such were the main points covered in the contract. That night, Omoto and Tsugami took Tashiro to a nice Japanese restaurant in Kyoto. The following night, Tashiro returned the favor by taking them and a few of the paper's directors to a sukiyaki place in Osaka's black market and buying everyone round after round of sake.

"I'm not a superstitious man," he said, "but I thought sukiyaki might be just the thing, even if it is in somewhat poor taste. Either way, we're going to get fat off these cows!"

Tashiro was in high spirits, thrilled at how well things had turned out. Soon the sake started going to his head, and he proposed that when the bulls reached Kobe they ought to dress them in really showy aprons, those ceremonial things worn by sumo wrestlers, and parade them along the streets from Kobe to Nishinomiya, and then the next day they could have another parade in Osaka, to kick things off in the grandest possible manner. He rubbed his oily face with his palm, then bent to fill Omoto's and Tsugami's cups. At moments like these, Tsugami was struck by the childlike look on Tashiro's face.

When Tashiro went off to use the restroom, Omoto, who had been as drunkenly giddy as the rest of them, declared in an oddly solemn tone, "The problem is all the money we'll have to sink into this thing until cash comes in from ticket sales. I did some rough calculations, and it looks to me like we'll need about a million yen."

"Yeah, it'll take that much for sure."

"So what do we do?"

"Oh, we'll find it somehow."

"You think?"

"We'll link all the publicity to advertising, and I'll find some way to convince the stadium to wait until after the event for the rental fees. The only worry is, we'll need two to three hundred thousand yen just to build the ring and the stable."

"We can't get three hundred thousand, not all at once!"

"It'll be all right, just leave it to me."

Tsugami had no clear plan in mind, but if all else failed they could raise the cash by selling tickets in advance. Right now his thoughts were focused less on financial details than on the parade of bulls that Tashiro had suggested. Twenty or so bulls. It would make an eye-catching article, nice photos. At the very least it was sure to get everyone talking. Somewhere deep in his head, which was throbbing a bit now from the mixture of sake and whiskey, he kept carefully sketching out that marvelous scene, then erasing it; sketching it, and erasing it.

The next day, Tsugami formed a Bullfighting Tournament Preparation Committee. He appointed as its members T., who couldn't write a newspaper article to save his life but had an extraordinary talent for negotiating; M., who came up with great ideas but couldn't carry them out; and a few other young men from advertising.

Only two months remained until the date of the tournament. The first announcement would have to appear in the paper at least a month in advance, which meant running it in the middle of December. The arrangements would have to be finished by then. Bargaining with the stadiums could wait; first they needed to get the bulls. And so, just two or three days after Tashiro went back to Shikoku, Tsugami and the young reporter T. made the trip down to W. As it turned out, by the time they arrived Tashiro had already done all the necessary negotiating with the locals and the Association—they had agreed to a bull-rental fee of twenty thousand a head and selected twenty-two glorious bulls for the ring; there was nothing left for Tsugami and T. to do. Naturally the Association and the owners were as enthusiastic as could be, and treated Tsugami and T. with such reverence—almost like two messiahs—that they wondered how Tashiro had talked them up.

The owners were all wealthy locals; it appeared that in this region it was everyone's dream to be rich enough one day to possess a sumo bull. People who, had they lived anywhere else in the country, would have built themselves a grand storehouse spent their money instead on massive animals bred purely for bullfighting, and they had been doing so for ages.

Tsugami and the others paid a visit to the house of Atomiya Shigesaburō, an old man who served as vice-president of the Association and who was himself the owner of one of the bulls selected for the tournament. Atomiya, who was the most successful farmer in the region, was almost maniacal in his devotion to bullfighting; already in his seventies, he had the robust, hearty air of an aged warrior. Evidently he had inherited his craze for bullfighting from his father, who was such a bull-sumo fiend that, according to the truth-is-better-than-fiction story people told, his last words as he lay on his deathbed had been, "I made my fortune, I built this house, so I have no real regrets. The one regret I have is that my bull always lost to Tamura's. Avenge me, son."

Naturally Atomiya, who was still young at the time, devoted himself with all the energy he could muster to training the family bull, in accordance with his father's dying wish. At the April tournament three years after his father passed away, the story goes, the bull upon which he had lavished so much attention and love finally took down Tamura's bull, and Atomiya tied his father's picture to the bull's back and paraded the animal in its slow, rocking way through the streets of W.

Listening as the old man slowly told his stories on that first night, the haori and hakama he wore giving him an air so formal that he might have been welcoming the prefectural governor to his house, Tsugami felt himself flirting oddly with depression, his gloom strengthened by his exhaustion after the lengthy trip. It wasn't old man Atomiya who had this effect on him; for some reason, whenever he felt the heat of the bull fever that gripped this region radiating across his face, his heart would sink rather than rise to match the excitement around him. Each morning as he sat on the verandah at the inn, facing the undulating azure sea, its color vivid and intense in the way it only ever is in the south, he would stare out over the water, struggling not to give in to some feeling he could not define.

Tashiro was busy the whole time Tsugami and T. were in town. He took the two visitors to see the shrine where the bull-sumo tournament was held each January, showed them the major bull stables scattered throughout W. and its environs, and then on the way back made a detour to lead them past a house where he said his brother lived, which was ringed by a stone wall—a rarity in the countryside. Everywhere they went he wore his heavy leather overcoat and rushed about in a hurry, the tip of his nose glistening with sweat. Almost every night there was a party, which he would inaugurate by saying a few words, calling Tsugami and the reporter T. "Sensei" and sometimes referring to the *New Evening Post* as "our company," as though he himself were an employee.

As soon as Tsugami returned to Osaka, he got started on the next stage of activities. Everything had gone smoothly in W., but here he met with one unexpected hitch after the next. First there was the all-important matter of booking a venue. Only one of the two stadiums in the area, Hanshin Stadium, would be available around the time they needed it, and after they had already concluded negotiations for use of the building during a three-day period starting January 20, just as they were on the verge of signing the contract, the other side started making difficulties. According to Naniwa Railway, which owned the stadium, the place had long had a reputation for being harder to play baseball in than the other stadium, which was owned by a rival railway company. After the war they had done everything possible to upgrade the field, hoping to wipe away once and for all this negative image, and they were damned if they were going to let anyone come in and hammer stakes into it now, and erect some big round bamboo fence, and have bulls kicking holes in it with their dirty hooves. They were right to object. After any number of determined exchanges, the two sides finally reached a tentative agreement that would enable the paper to rent the stadium, but no sooner had they heaved a sigh of relief at that than the pro baseball team that played in the stadium started grousing because they wouldn't be able to play during that period. The paper barely managed to mollify the players by asking two or three big-boss types to intervene, but it took a shocking sum of money to make it happen. And then the prefectural Safety Division refused to grant permission for the event. The reason they gave was that the form of entertainment known as "bullfighting" had no history in Japan, so there was no protocol for dealing with it. The paper telegrammed Tashiro to come up right away from Shikoku, only to learn that even in Ehime Prefecture, the original birthplace of bull sumo, permission had never once been granted to present the sport as an entertainment. Omoto went to talk to the authorities, Tsugami went to talk to the authorities, but even after endless wrangling back and forth the authorities still refused to budge. Meanwhile Tashiro, who had made the trip between Shikoku and Osaka three times, began building support in Ehime by asking prominent local figures for help. After all this had failed, the reporter T., with his genius for negotiating, took over. He paid a few visits to the Prefectural Office, provided a signed statement explaining that in the event of an accident they would immediately cancel the entire tournament, and came back having persuaded the chief of the Safety Division to approve the bullfight. That had been just two or three days ago. And now here it was—the draft for the notice announcing the tournament, which Tsugami had almost given up on ever seeing in print, laid out by a young man in the copyediting department, right there on the front page: two bulls ramming their heads together, cut out of a photograph, inserted into a large box right between the day's two lead stories, one about a teacher's strike and another about infighting in the Socialist Party, where it would catch anyone's eye. To Omoto and Tsugami both, the ad was like a hunting dog that had broken free from their grasp.

*

Tashiro walked for two blocks along a road like a gash in the burned-out ruins, feeling the wind first at his back and then hitting him from the front so he had to lean into it; then, suddenly, he stopped before a half-destroyed building, raised his right hand slightly in a signal to Tsugami that this was it, and plunged through a doorway one could easily have missed and on down a stairway that led belowground.

In part because his motions were so exaggerated, it seemed as if Tashiro had simply disappeared, just like that, from the earth's surface. Tsugami followed behind, proceeding one step at a time down a dim flight of steps so narrow he could barely squeeze through. Arriving at the bottom after turning a corner partway down, he found himself in a surprisingly wide room, brightly illuminated by numerous electric bulbs. In the center there were a few shrubs and even a stone lantern, suggesting a traditional Japanese-style garden, and around the garden were four neat little rooms with tatami floors, each one a separate structure, still in the process of being built. One was being made into a bar, judging from the tall, narrow-backed chairs stacked in the corner with a few blue-painted beer barrels. Four men stood before the barrels, rotating a tiled sink this way and that, working on installing it in the washroom.

In another small room at the back, the only one that was about ninety percent done, Okabe Yata sat at a kotatsu with a half-empty bottle of whiskey before him on the tabletop, a padded kimono over his drab wartime "national uniform."

"Hey, come on in!"

By the time Tsugami had time to sit down, Okabe had already peeled off his padded kimono and was warmly bowing his head. He looked rather insubstantial with his diminutive stature and his small face, which filled with tiny wrinkles when he spoke, but something in his casual affability suggested on the contrary that he possessed a certain brashness, a willingness to walk right over other people.

"I've been waiting for you, Mr. Tsugami!"

Tsugami, staring at Okabe's thin lips, which moved quite a lot when he spoke, felt slightly turned off by the man's attitude—so familiar you half expected him to reach out and pat you on the shoulder. Tsugami held out his business card the same way he always would, behaving if anything more stiffly than usual.

Okabe removed his business-card holder from his pocket and felt around inside, then snapped his fingers to call over a young man who seemed to be his secretary.

"Write out a business card for him, will you?" he said, passing the man a notepad and a fountain pen. "Put down the company phone."

He picked up Tsugami's card and held it out to Tashiro, who explained what it said: that Tsugami was the editor-in-chief of a newspaper. Okabe nodded a few times but said nothing. Tsugami looked once more at the small, unremarkable man who sat before him with an air that somehow suggested he wasn't afraid of anything. Unless Tsugami's acumen had failed him, Okabe, who Tashiro had said was the most successful man from Iyo, was unable either to read or to write.

Someone brought drinks and food. Okabe adeptly kept up a constant stream of talk, his attitude open and informal. "I'm thinking of turning this into kind of a space for people to indulge themselves, see? We Japanese have been starved for good food, so my idea is to make this the place you come to for absolutely the best of the best. When we open, I'll introduce you to three of the top cooks from Beppu, Kōchi, and Akita. Come see me, all right?"

Tashiro had become so rigid in front of Okabe that it was funny. His hefty frame was completely engulfed by Okabe's small body, all of one hundred and fifty centimeters tall. He didn't say a word about the important matter he had brought Tsugami and Okabe together to discuss, but just went on taking the dishes as they were carried out and arranging them on the table, grabbing the bottle and filling the men's glasses the second they were empty. When he wasn't doing this, he sat there meekly, unobtrusively, listening as though he didn't want to miss a word they said.

Tsugami waited with a certain amount of curiosity for Okabe to come out and say what was on his mind. He himself wasn't a heavy drinker by any means, but each time his cup was filled he raised it to his lips. Right about now, newspaper boys would be walking around the streets distributing the paper with the announcement of the tournament.

"Does company work keep you busy?" Tsugami asked.

"Not at all, nothing to do. I've got five or six companies, but to tell the truth, yeah, I have a lot of time on my hands. Can't expect a company to thrive if the president is busy, you know? I just sit here drinking like this day after day, that's all they need from me."

Okabe had a penchant for taking his listeners by surprise, and he seemed to enjoy it. Evidently at the moment he was less concerned with figuring out what sort of man his new acquaintance Tsugami was than with expressing his own sense of himself.

"Seriously, I'm not kidding! You can't hope for much from a person's mind until you pour in some booze. You can wrack your brains all you like when you're sober, but you still won't turn up anything worth having, you know?" From time to time, as Okabe spoke, his small eyes would sparkle and he would peer into Tsugami's so long and hard it was almost rude—an effect, perhaps, of all the whiskey he had downed before they arrived. He kept his tumbler in his hand as he talked, sometimes tossing down a few glasses of the yellow liquid in a row, holding it in his mouth for a moment before swallowing, his face expressionless.

"So. Let me tell you how I got where I am, Mr. Tsugami—you too, Tashiro."

"By all means, please! I've always wanted to ask. The Making of the Great Okabc."

Tashiro was so abject in his pandering to Okabe that it put Tsugami off. Tashiro reached out to pour Okabe more whiskey; rather than hold his tumbler out, Okabe simply pushed it along the table. He sat for a few moments with his small eyes shut, a smug expression on his face, and then suddenly snapped his eyelids open.

"I don't know if I'm the Great Okabe or the Little Okabe or what. I can tell you, though, all these companies I've got, I built them all up after the war ended. Be nice if I could say I've accomplished it all in one generation, but the truth is I did it in a year, out of nothing. One year, that's all. That's what makes this world so much fun. How fast things change." He laughed hoarsely.

Okabe had returned from the South Seas in the November after the war ended, about a year ago. He was thirty-eight when he was called up, forty-two when he came back. He had no wife and no children. He borrowed three thousand yen from a woman he had been involved with almost a decade earlier and fled from his hometown in Iyo, coming up to Kobe to shack up with a friend from his soldier days who had a job driving a truck. After lazing about for half a month, he decided that he could make some money selling farm equipment.

He had heard that a company called Akebono Manufacturing in Amagasaki had produced a new kind of thresher with an electric motor, and hit upon the idea of finding some way to acquire a whole bunch of these things and then sell them off—it was the perfect way to sponge up some of the cash that had been flooding into the farming villages of late. The first thing he did was go have a talk with the management at Akebono Manufacturing, introducing himself with a business card that identified him as "Director, Akebono Industrial Co." Needless to say it was fake: he'd had the cards printed a few days earlier at a department store in Osaka. His little ploy had precisely the desired effect. Well look at that, your company's called Akebono, too! The coincidence of the two names created a sort of connection, predisposing the men at Akebono Manufacturing toward him, and as a result they agreed to go ahead and ship a hundred threshers to him the very next day. The contract was extraordinarily generous by usual business standards—they would let him pay the following day, when the goods arrived. So now the only problem was how to come up with the three hundred thousand yen he had to hand over when the goods arrived.

"So how do you think I got the three hundred grand? I borrowed it from a stranger."

Okabe's tone, as he spoke these two brief sentences, sounded oddly intense and sharp in comparison with his usual tone. He had set his sights on a man named Yamamoto, a former Diet member from the same prefecture who had made a fortune doing business with the military, and decided that come what may he would find a way to get three hundred thousand yen out of him. He went straight from Akebono Manufacturing to Yamamoto's house in Mikage and cajoled and pleaded with the man to lend him three hundred thousand yen as a favor to a child of the same prefecture, but to no avail—obviously there had never been any chance that Yamamoto would agree. Okabe visited Yamamoto's house three times that day, and on the third he finally sat down on the packed dirt floor of the entryway and refused to budge, only to be struck by a sudden, almost mystical flash of inspiration: he would take out a three-hundred-thousand-yen life insurance policy and use the contract as security.

Without waiting another moment he rushed off to N. Life, which was operating from a temporary location in the burned-out area around Yodoyabashi, but by the time he arrived it was evening and the office was closed. He had no choice but to ask the employee keeping watch to look up the home address of the insurance section chief and then go off and barge into his house in Suita, asking for a three-hundred-thousand-yen contract. The insurance section chief's response was negative: I can't do it today, you'll have to come by the office tomorrow. Ah, I'm afraid that won't work, Okabe told him, and with that they entered into a long series of exchanges that finally ended with Okabe getting exactly what he wanted. He handed over three thousand yen and went away that same evening with a provisional contract worth three hundred thousand yen. He got on one of the last trains, went back to Yamamoto's house, and pushed as hard as he possibly could, telling him he had the life insurance contract right here to use as security, so wouldn't he please just lend him the money?

"And it worked. In retrospect, of course, a life insurance contract isn't worth anything. But that's what makes people so fascinating! The way he saw it, I was putting my life on the line. So he said, 'All right, if you're that determined I'll lend you the money for a month, that's all.' And that was how I got started doing what I do now."

Tsugami found it difficult to fathom Okabe's true intentions in recounting his past adventures as a swindler—since that was what it was—but the tale didn't bore him. Okabe's tone had in it a sort of self-absorption that was almost passionate.

"Interesting story," Tsugami said, not entirely out of politeness.

"Anyway, that's basically the kind of guy I am. Only now I've got ten or twenty million yen in my pocket. So how about it, Mr. Tsugami? You think I might be able to help out with this bullfighting thing your paper is planning?"

Tsugami, caught off guard, locked eyes with Okabe

for a moment; Okabe glanced away, took his time lighting a cigarette, and then turned to face Tsugami again. There was a stony, insistent glare in his eyes that said he would not give up easily.

"If you don't want to buy the bulls as a joint investment, I'll buy them all myself. I'll also assume all the shipping costs, the costs associated with the tournament, and everything else relating to the bulls. You run the project without having to pay a thing, turn as much of a profit as you like." Okabe's voice was quiet but his tone made it clear he would brook no opposition.

"I'm afraid that won't work," Tsugami said, once Okabe had said his piece.

Tsugami couldn't argue with the fact that accepting his proposal would result in a sweet deal for the newspaper, even if Okabe's character made him slightly uneasy. But he had been seized with an intense dislike for those two little eyes, brimming with confidence, that were now trained upon him. He felt agitated, as if he and Okabe were engaged in a duel, and the motions of his spirit drained his face ever so slightly of its color, infusing it with a look of elation.

"No, I think the paper had better manage this on its own. This is my first project of this type, after all."

Okabe held his tumbler and listened, nodding politely. Then, when Tsugami had finished, he let the subject drop surprisingly easily: "I see. Yes indeed. Well, too bad, but I guess it can't be helped."

He poured Tsugami another glass of whiskey, as if to change his mood.

"I must say," he boomed as he poured, "I like you. I like your style. You're absolutely right, this is your idea, your job. Of course you should do it on your own! To tell you the truth, I feel even better now that you've turned me down."

You couldn't tell how sincere Okabe was being, but he did seem in high spirits.

It had felt like night in the basement room, with all the electric lighting; when they stepped outside again, a winter dusk was just beginning to drape itself over the charred, burned-out strip.

"Why did you refuse?" Tashiro said, running up behind Tsugami. "What a waste!"

"Yes, it's a waste."

Tsugami didn't need Tashiro to tell him; he was thinking the same thing. The two men turned up the collars of their overcoats and walked shoulder to shoulder; then, as they stepped to the side of the road to avoid a passing truck and briefly stood facing each other, Tashiro spoke.

"Perhaps I should have mentioned this earlier. Actually, we have a bit of a problem."

Eight railway cars were needed to move twenty-two bulls, but at present only two were leaving W. each day. Obviously they couldn't proceed with just two, so Tashiro had been negotiating with the Hiroshima Railway Bureau for special permission to extend the train; so far, however, he had made no headway. The authorities had pointed out that the timing was bad in terms of the availability of coal, and in any event they simply didn't have any extra cars. Tsugami walked on in silence. He felt as if he were looking at the ocean, watching another enormous whitecap heave itself up as it rushed toward the shore.

"Under the circumstances," Tashiro said, "I don't think we have any choice but to ask Okabe to use his business connections, get him to talk with the Railway Bureau, and convince them to find some way around this. That's the only solution."

Tsugami stopped in his tracks and cast an accusatory glance at Tashiro.

"You'd already told him, hadn't you."

Tashiro smirked. "He's quite a man. You turn him down, and still he wants to step in and give us a helping hand."

Tsugami really had no desire to be on the receiving end of a helping hand or even a helping finger from Okabe, but he understood that it was already too late: without his realizing it, that small, fearless man had insinuated himself into the bullfighting tournament. Obviously Tashiro had already been to see Okabe about this problem, and that business about buying the bulls was his bargaining chip.

*

Sakiko had not paid a visit to Tsugami since the calendar returned to January. From late autumn into the New Year, Tsugami had spent almost every night at the office, abandoning even a planned visit to his parents' house in rural Tottori so that he could keep dashing around taking care of preparations for the bullfight. The one exception had been the last day of the year, when Sakiko insisted that they go hear the temple bells being struck, and he agreed, and they went up to Kyoto and spent the night at an inn in Okazaki they had been to before, in a room so quiet that if you sat still you could hear the water coursing in the canal.

The past two or three days had been blustery, but that evening the wind died down and the stars were gorgeous. At midnight, all at once, the long, low gonging of the bells began issuing for the first time in years from all the great temples scattered throughout the city. Even Tsugami, who had been crouched over the low desk sipping the whiskey he had brought with him, carefully writing out in his brand-new pocket-size diary everything that needed to be done in the twenty days remaining until the tournament, set down his pen and surrendered to the sound. Sakiko sat beside him. They heard the bells being struck at regular intervals, nearby and far away, their countless reverberations all layering and colliding, echoing into each other, flowing like a hundred streams through the crisp midnight air.

They sat for a long time, saying nothing. It was a peculiarly quiet moment, unlike any Sakiko had experienced in all the years she and Tsugami had been together. The face of this man, liberated now from his work, as if some possessing spirit had lost its hold on him, looked oddly plain and docile. Oh, look at him—that helpless face, she thought. And suddenly, like water spreading through her, she felt something that was neither love nor hatred, but a sense of how truly lost he would be without her. It was a pure feeling, far removed from desire. Again and again, endlessly, the bells rang.

The bells would be struck one hundred and eight times. A little past the halfway mark, Tsugami got to his feet, opened the window, and stood for a time looking out. Sakiko rose, too, then went and leaned against him. Outside the night was uncannily dark and deep, nothing but the sound of the bells flying past. Thick foliage walled them in, blocking out every trace of light from the town. All at once, Sakiko felt intensely uneasy. The very fact that they were standing here quietly beside one another, as much like two lovers as two lovers could be, listening to the passing of the ringing of the bells being struck to send off the old year, filled her with a dark sense of foreboding. Maybe the only reason we are able to share a night like this, she thought, is that this time we really are going to break up.

Sakiko stepped away from Tsugami and went to sit at the small red-lacquered mirror in the corner. Her heart was still pounding. In the mirror, staring out at her like a fox, was the ashen face of a woman who had spent three years of the most important period in her life, from her twenties into her thirties, suffering with Tsugami.

*

Partly because of what felt like the onset of a cold, Sakiko spent the unseasonably warm first days of the new year holed up in her apartment. As soon as the three-day holiday ended, the *New Evening Post* started running a remarkable number of articles about bullfighting. One day there was an interview on the subject with a celebrated opera singer known for his performance of José in *Carmen*, and then the next a large section of a page was devoted to bullfighting anecdotes that Count F., a well-known sports enthusiast, had shared with the paper. One article, accompanied by a photograph, introduced an old sculptor who specialized in fighting bulls; in another, printed under the rather pedantic headline "The Specialist's View," an up-and-coming boxer offered his thoughts on the nature of the sport. They also ran a special series called "A Visit to the Fighting Bulls in the Nan'yo Region."

Sakiko was not in the least interested in bullfighting, but this incessant stream of articles, day after day, inspired in her the same feeling she got looking into Tsugami's coldly blazing eyes, so passionate he seemed like a man possessed. The angles the articles took were so typical of him; spread there on the page, they were like a map of his neuroses, his likes, his idiosyncratic style. One introduced an old man in W. who had worked as a handler in the ring for thirty years and had been recruited to serve as a commentator for the tournament; another outlined plans news media in Japan and elsewhere in the world had to film the event—though they were treated as news, in essence they were advertisements, meant to drum up interest. Reading them, Sakiko could imagine Tsugami running around, coming up with new ideas, working out plans, negotiating.

On the 8th, she decided to go see him. Once she had made up her mind she found it impossible to sit still. She would have to go back to the dressmaking shop in Shinsaibashi where she worked the next day, and besides, that unease she had felt on New Year's Eve was still there like a knot inside her, even now that a new year had begun.

She called the newspaper and learned that for the past few days Tsugami had been working from Hanshin Stadium, where the tournament would be held, and staying over at a hotel in the area. And so, though he had warned her repeatedly never, under any circumstances, to come to see him at work, she went to Hanshin Stadium. The day was cold, the sunlight pale; one had the sense that snowflakes might start fluttering down at any minute. She got off the train at Nishinomiya Kitaguchi. She always saw the stadium from the train, but this was the first time she had ever been inside the vast, round, modern structure. She walked through the massive emptiness of the bowl to the other side and went in and to the left, and there was the office: a cramped room like a ship's cabin that seemed entirely out of place in a building so large.

When she opened the door, four or five men who could have been from the paper or just visiting, she couldn't tell, were gathered around a lit charcoal brazier, puffing away on their cigarettes. Beyond them was Tsugami: he was talking loudly to someone on the phone on the desk, the receiver pressed against his ear, the collar of his overcoat turned up. The cool, accusatory glance he shot at Sakiko when he noticed her standing in the doorway was like a knife in her heart. When he finally finished his long phone call, he stood and strode out of the room. He walked ahead of her up the dim, gently sloping concrete corridor, which turned back on itself, then turned back again, zigzagging upward in a shape like a bolt of cartoon lightning, his angry footsteps echoing through the building. On the fourth floor, he walked through the passageway to the stands and stopped just outside to wait.

"Why are you here? What do you need?" he said finally, as she came out.

His cheeks were wan, and he had lost a lot of weight. He glared at her for just a second with a look that could kill, then looked away. He always looked at her like that when he was in a bad mood.

"Am I only allowed to come if I need something?" she asked, trying to sound casual. She glanced up at him, keeping her face down, burying the lower half in her navy overcoat. If she wasn't careful, she might say something harsh. They were in the infield stands, on the uppermost level; down below, as far as they could see, the vast, deserted stadium was filled with shoddily installed wooden seats that formed bleak stripes as they fell away step by step toward the playing field at the center. The wind was strong, perhaps because they were so high up; the weak afternoon sun gave the entire gray building a rough and gritty appearance.

"I told you how insanely busy I am, right?"

"Please, this is the first time I've seen you this year. Don't look at me in that scary way, like I have no business being here. Is that the kind of relationship we have?"

"Don't start with that again. I'm too tired." Tsugami's tone was so stony she didn't know how to reply. She stood directly in front of him, equally pale, peering up at him as he sulkily put a cigarette in his mouth. The chill wind tousled his hair. The way they were standing made them seem almost like two men facing off in a duel; realizing this, he told her to sit down, then immediately lowered himself on to the nearest bench. She sat down next to him.

Around the stadium, to the west and to the east, as far as the eye could see, dead fields extended into the distance. During the war, all the major munitions factories in Osaka and Kobe had relocated here to this wide plain between the cities; from here, the buildings looked oddly weightless, like scraps of paper dotting the vast landscape. One resembled a shipwrecked boat with its steel beams jutting up into the sky; another had a small mountain of scrap iron out in the yard. When you actually looked at the scene, you were struck by how many smokestacks and electric poles there were, and by all the wires crisscrossing the field like spider silk. Every now and then a suburban train, small as a toy, would pass by, weaving its way among the factories, the woods, the hills. Off in the distance, to the northeast, you could see the Rokkō mountain range. And then there was the overcast sky, hanging low over the desolate, wintry expanse of land and its haphazard mixture of industrial mess and natural severity.

Sakiko let her eyes roam across the frozen scenery, saying nothing, but in her heart she was already plumbing the depths of the pain Tsugami's iciness would cause her after they had parted. She realized, at this almost absurdly late stage in the game, that all she had really wanted from Tsugami was a little love, just a scrap, to warm herself by—that was the only reason she had come. A few gentle words were all she needed; they didn't even have to be true. Even the cruelest, most insincere display of affection would make her happy. She stared at the face of the man who sat beside her, utterly unconnected to her agony. All at once, a fresh sense of rage bubbled up within her at his unwillingness even to make the effort to deceive himself, and in her rage, for no other reason than that the thought had occurred to her, her tone as flat as if she were demanding the repayment of a loan, she told him that a friend in Kyoto had invited them to a tea ceremony at a temple, at Ninnaji, and she wanted to go. He didn't reply. His expression registered his disbelief.

"It's the 14th. Just that one day."

"There's no way."

"Just the afternoon, then—half a day."

"It's impossible. Until the bullfight is over, I really can't do anything."

With that, his moody expression softened: a placard descended over his face that announced that this woman beside him was his lover, even now. Anyway, he said, he'd be damned if he was going to make the trip all the way up to Ninnaji, like he had all the time in the world.

"It seems negotiations have broken down," Sakiko said hoarsely. "Stupid of me even to suggest it when I knew you would just push me away."

"I'm not pushing you away."

"Oh really? Is that what you think?" A sudden flash of anger at his coldness crushed her restraint. "Go on and push me, then! Give me a push so hard I'll go rolling down those benches like a ball! I'd love to see the look on your face as I go tumbling down."

They fell silent. Her anger faded, leaving her with nothing more to say, and an irredeemable sense of sorrow diffused itself slowly through her heart, like a shadow crossing the surface of a pond. One of them would have to get up; there was no other way to break this awkward impasse.

After a moment, Tsugami said he had remembered something he had to do and left for the office. Five minutes later he came hurrying back out and explained that he still had three or four tasks left to take care of today, and it would be like this every day until the tournament. Maybe they could take a trip to one of the hot springs in Kishū or something, as soon as the bullfight was over. There was a hint of kindness in his tone that had not been there before.

"Everything keeps going awry," he said, as if he wanted to make her understand. "All our plans are falling apart."

He pointed to a white ring drawn in the center of the field and told her that they needed to erect a bamboo enclosure there, a ring thirty-five meters in diameter, and even that, something as simple as that, wasn't going at all smoothly. They had asked someone from the Bull Sumo Association to come up as soon as he could to supervise the construction of the ring, and he came, but then the bamboo didn't materialize. It had finally arrived this morning, but now it seemed the all-important supervisor had come down with a cold the day before and couldn't get out of bed. Sakiko could see that he was telling the truth: he had been dealing with an overwhelming amount of business. The phone call he had been making when she turned up at the office had been about the fireworks they were planning to send up over Nakanoshima Park the night before the tournament: they had already negotiated for permission, but now for some reason that permission had been retracted. The town authorities were hesitant because this would be the first aerial firework display since the end of the war, and of course rules governing the use of gunpowder were very strict; they would do what they could to help, but they couldn't say for certain that permission would be granted as a matter of course.

"I can't give up on those fireworks, though. That's the one thing. We're going to have dozens of strings of firecrackers going off during the day, so I'd really like to send up a few fireworks at night, too, something showy."

Tsugami's irritation was plainly written on his face.

"Yes, that would be lovely. Maybe you can do a big chrysanthemum! How nice it will look blooming in the total darkness over the charred rubble of Osaka."

Sakiko had promised herself she wouldn't say another word, but somehow this bit of irony slipped out. Please don't tell me he wants to have them go up in the shape of a cow, she thought. But then she noticed how earnest he looked, as if that might be exactly what he had in mind, and all at once her mood rocked. In her mind's eye she saw Tsugami's face, raised toward the doubly black darkness that follows a burst of fireworks—a face that only she knew, and that felt, somehow, soothingly cool.

The men waiting for him in the office right now, Tsugami went on to say, were from the printer, a transport company, and a funeral parlor. They were wrangling over costs with all three companies, and the men had come to talk things over, but it was starting to look as though no progress would be made unless he took them out drinking. The man from the funeral parlor was there because he used part of his gasoline rations to operate a number of sound trucks. He was going to dispatch his trucks all around Osaka and Kobe to advertise the tournament.

"These sound trucks, each one loaded with comedians and revue girls, a record player, they come barreling out of the same garage as the hearses headed for the crematory, and it's the same company—can you believe that?" Tsugami said, without so much as a smile. "Not that there's anything wrong with that, exactly..."

Sakiko understood now how overworked and frazzled he was. At the same time, she didn't fail to notice that despite his dejected tone, he was also—in a manner entirely characteristic of him—feeling a bit giddy, inextricably caught up as he was in these rather shady business dealings, the not-quite-right incidents, all so emblematic of this confused age, fighting against the odds to make things work.

Standing on the platform at Nishinomiya Kitaguchi Station, waiting for the train to Osaka, Sakiko could not have felt more different from when she had come. Her body and heart were both so cold nothing could have warmed them. She was leaning on the wooden fence, her head wrapped up in her muffler, when it occurred to her that this bullfight of Tsugami's might be a total failure. The thought burst in her mind like a flash of lightning out of the blue. Shivering uncontrollably, she kept feeling that premonition, so strong it was almost a conviction, kept feeling that he was headed for disaster, he was going to fail, seeing him in her mind's eye, turned away from him, looking very cold, just as he had earlier, when they had parted ways, and she couldn't tell whether the emotion that welled in her breast was affection or a wish to see him destroyed.

*

The bullfighting tournament was only ten days away, and both the front and second pages of the *Osaka New Evening Post* were now covered with articles relating to it. This was one of the advantages of being a small evening paper—a more prominent newspaper could not easily have set aside space to publicize one of its own enterprises, while the *New Evening Post* could eliminate all the news it wanted, as long as it wasn't too significant, replacing each article with publicity. They used photos of bulls' heads in the picture box that went with the editorial, and bullfighting made an appearance in a popular comic strip they serialized. Tsugami kept hearing that the sarcastic fellows over at *B. News* had been mocking him, saying he had started putting out a cowspaper, but he and Omoto acted as if they hadn't heard a thing—they would go on publishing their cowspaper right up to the day of the tournament, no matter what anyone said. No sooner had they published the prize-winning Bullfighting Tournament Theme Song than they ran an announcement soliciting fighting names for the twenty-two bulls who would participate in the great event. The same day, a young reporter proposed that they let people vote on which bull they expected to win—a plan the reporter himself worried might be a bit too much, but which Tsugami instantly approved. At times like these, Tsugami would sit briefly with his cigarette dangling from his mouth, a far-off, unfocused look in his eyes, and then all of a sudden, so quickly it was hard to see how he could have had time to think, he would issue his decision in a somewhat shrill tone. He gave the impression less that he had thought things through than that he had been struck by an almost divine inspiration. As the tournament approached and the number of little tasks he had to take care of kept increasing, he grew progressively less talkative and more active.

At the same time all this was going on, a rather flashy advertising campaign was unfolding in other venues, apart from the paper itself, largely as a result of the young reporter T.'s efforts. Large, well-placed posters depicting two bulls locking horns caught the gazes of the crowds gathered in the bus terminals and subway stations of Umeda, Naniwa, Ueroku. Small posters with the exact same design hung in every bus and in every car of every suburban train. Once they had held a ceremony to introduce the Bullfighting Tournament Theme Song at a certain theater in Shinsaibashi, they started sending the sound trucks around to the now colder-than-ever shantytowns, the song blaring from the microphones on their roofs. Day after day, three trucks drove around Osaka and two around Kobe, each stocked with a supply of dancing girls.

The expenses associated with these activities greatly exceeded expectations, and, when the costs of building the ring and the stable were added, the financial burden was considerably heavier than the *Osaka New Evening Post* could bear. The accountants were the first to raise the alarm. They drastically reduced allowable expenses for travel, parties, and miscellaneous costs, and ended the almost openly acknowledged system of payday loans, tolerated in silence by the higher-ups as a temporary means of alleviating the penury of the paper's employees. They even announced that payment of the night-shift allowance, normally distributed on the 15th, would be delayed until the end of the month. When the notice announcing this was posted on the bulletin board, the chief of the accounting department came to see Tsugami and drive home in a rather painful way how serious this was.

"Mr. Tsugami, I can't have you spending any more on this, I really can't. Many of our employees rely on the night-shift allowance."

Three days before the tournament, Tsugami received a telegraph from Tashiro that read: "SIX A.M. TOMORROW BULLS ARRIVE NISHINOMIYA." The stable where the twenty-two bulls would be kept was ready, having been built in a barren area across from Nishinomiya Station; the hundred-plus people who had been brought into town, including the bulls' owners and handlers, had all been assigned to lodges and inns in Nishinomiya that had survived the firebombings. That night, Omoto and Tsugami clinked whiskey glasses at a bar on Umeda Shinmichi frequented by Omoto.

"Well," Tsugami said, "at least we know the bulls will be here."

Relief showed on both men's faces.

"Tell me about it. Imagine if the train had gone missing or something—boy, would we have been screwed. I have to say, though, it sure cost a lot to get to this point."

Tsugami sensed a note of reproach in Omoto's voice, but he pretended he hadn't. "They say these days any project will cost five times what you think it will. We'll have done pretty well if we come out of this just three times over budget, I'd say."

"And we ought to be done with the big expenditures, now that we've come this far."

"I think so. Even if we do need more money, we'll figure something out."

"Spoken like a true reporter. Coming up with one or two hundred thousand yen isn't actually all that easy, you know."

Tsugami caught himself just as he was about to comment that if worst came to worst, Omoto had enough, didn't he? He restrained his irony and instead said quietly, "Five days from now, we'll have a million extra yen pouring in."

They were banking on an audience of thirty thousand each day, yielding a three-day total of about a hundred thousand. There would be five thousand fifty-yen ringside tickets, twenty thousand forty-yen infield tickets, and seventy-five thousand rear infield and outfield tickets that would go for thirty yen each. Total sales should come out to three million three hundred thousand yen; subtract a million for expenses and you were left with two million three hundred thousand in pure profit. After splitting the profits with Tashiro, the paper would take in about a million. That, at any rate, was how Tsugami had calculated it.

Omoto had a reputation both inside and outside the company as a generous, reckless manager, in contrast to Tsugami, who was known for keeping a tight rein on everything; somewhere along the way, though, the two men had swapped roles. They themselves saw this most clearly. Tsugami had noticed the unexpectedly nervy, calculating core concealed within Omoto's seemingly openhanded, nonchalant manner; Omoto, with all his years of experience taking stock of people, had noted with a certain unease that underneath his stern outer shell, this young reporter, reputed to be so sharp, so clearly fastidious, even picky, harbored a tendency to wallow half-wittedly in his desires that made it unwise to trust him too far.

*

The next morning Tsugami took the first train on the government line to Sannomiya Station, only to discover that the freight train had arrived at dawn, around four, about two hours earlier than Tashiro had expected, and the whole party was milling about in one corner of the train yard. The twenty-two magnificent bulls, each of which must have weighed over seven hundred and fifty kilograms, stood with their handlers, tied to the station's wooden fence, steam rising from their bodies. Tashiro, who had been with a group of men surrounding a bonfire near the freight house, strode over looking cold, chin tucked into his leather overcoat. As he approached, he jubilantly cried out, "Ah, Mr. Tsugami! What do you think?" He nodded toward the bulls. "Splendid, aren't they! They're not like these cows in Kobe and Osaka, fed on leftovers."

Standing there with a cigarette in his mouth, not bothering to say good morning or even to take his hands out of his pockets, Tashiro had the unmistakable air of a showman, elated at his success.

"Rough morning, I bet."

"Actually no, the ride was surprisingly relaxing—having the whole train to ourselves made things easy. Sure took a long time, though, one night here, next night somewhere else. Five days, including today. I'm exhausted, let me tell you."

So he said. He didn't look particularly exhausted to Tsugami.

And sure enough, the next instant he was ready for business. "So we're all set for the parade?"

They had arranged to depart from Sannomiya at eight, make the rounds of downtown Kobe, and deliver the parade of sumo bulls to the stable in Nishinomiya. The next morning they would walk them from Nishinomiya to Osaka, circle through the center of city, then return to Nishinomiya. Tsugami was anxious above all that the bulls might not be in good condition after so much rocking on the train, but Tashiro didn't seem concerned.

"They haven't exercised for so long, a bit of walking will be good for them."

Tashiro glanced up at the sky to gauge the weather, looked down at his watch, and then strode off with the contented gait of an officer inspecting his troops, saying he should at least peek in to thank the station manager for his help.

Tsugami was walking around greeting some of the owners who had helped with things during that first trip to W. when N., a reporter who had made the trip up on the train with the rest of the group, drew him aside, saying he had some information to pass on. "Look," he said, glancing meaningfully toward the far western edge of the yard, where the only opening in the fence allowed passage in and out. Four or five men were loading something into a truck. Tsugami noticed Tashiro among them;

he was standing next to the truck, evidently directing the men in their work.

"He brought that stuff up with us—says it's all feed for the bulls. A bunch of us are pretty sure he has something else going on, though. He's quite the huckster."

According to N., Tashiro had loaded an enormous number of mysterious bundles on to the train in W., each wrapped in straw mats and tightly tied, claiming that it was feed. N. was puzzled by the quantity, though, and when he looked inside one he discovered that it was stuffed with dried bonito. When he opened another, a stream of brown sugar gushed out.

"Feed for the bulls, my ass. And who knows what else is in there? Still, he's a crucial partner in this project, so I thought for the paper's sake I'd better just pretend I hadn't seen anything. And then in Takamatsu—it was hilarious, let me tell you."

There had been an earthquake in the ocean off Kishū while they were there, and it had bent the rails that delivered the cars on to the ferry. They had no choice but to unload the bulls and all the rest of the cargo from four of the eight cars, put everything on the boat, and then transfer it all to another set of cars in Uno. Even Tashiro had been rattled. He spent the whole day hurrying back and forth around Takamatsu, and then that night he had brought five or six men who unloaded the "feed" and took it off somewhere.

"The goods they're putting in the truck are what's left, the stuff from the four cars that made it on to the ferry."

N. was clearly furious, and proceeded to curse Tashiro roundly. Tsugami wasn't really surprised that an incident like this should have happened, but even so he felt a wave of displeasure rising up inside him as he stood there watching it happen. He walked up behind Tashiro where he stood near the truck and tapped the shoulder of his overcoat. When Tashiro looked around and saw that it was Tsugami, he suddenly broke into a broad grin.

"You're on to me," he said.

"How could I not be? You're doing it right out in the open."

"Well, you know," Tashiro murmured vaguely, then turned serious. "It's Mr. Okabe's stuff."

Tsugami noticed as Tashiro said this that the name of Okabe's company, Hanshin Manufacturing, was printed in white on the side of the truck. Tashiro had been unable to refuse. How could he say no when Okabe asked him to load up a few things and take them along, when without his help they would have been unable to get a single car and Okabe had gotten them eight? It just wasn't possible.

"Pretend you didn't see anything. He'll be useful to you again, trust me."

"I'm not sure I want him to be useful. A man like that..." Tsugami's expression was still sour.

"As it happens," Tashiro replied, "I'm afraid there's a little matter we're going to need his help on more or less immediately. We've got to feed the bulls."

For two or three days before a fight, you had to feed sumo bulls great heaps of rice and barley, and then on the actual day of the event you had to give them sake and eggs, too. If you were dealing with twenty-two bulls, well, you were going to need an awful lot of rice and barley, and so on. Tashiro had been planning to try and get special rations issued in Ehime, but in the end he hadn't been able to get permission, he said, though he had tried as hard as he could. And if they couldn't make it happen in Ehime, applying for rations in Hyōgo Prefecture or Osaka certainly wasn't going to work, since they were having trouble providing people with enough basic staple foods. When all was said and done, there didn't seem to be any choice but to beg Okabe for help.

"Ask him, and we'll have no problem getting feed

for twenty or even thirty bulls. It's only for two or three days, after all."

Even as he talked with Tsugami, Tashiro would occasionally shout at the men loading the truck—telling them to be careful, issuing instructions. Tsugami had begun feeling vaguely uneasy, as though, without his realizing it, someone had come and wound him up, around and around, with an invisible string. Now that he was feeling this way, he started noticing a certain nasty tinge to Tashiro's brazenness that hadn't been there before, as if he had decided he could get away with anything now.

"All right. I'll talk to Okabe," Tsugami said.

By the time Tsugami left Tashiro and rejoined the rest of the group, everyone from the paper who was involved with the tournament had arrived, and the air was buzzing with voices. He noticed one of the photographers rushing around taking pictures of the bulls. At seven, they started getting ready for the parade. As they were putting the showy sumo-style aprons over the bulls' backs, Tashiro, who always wore long pants, appeared wearing knickerbockers; he had replaced his usual overcoat with one that came down only to his waist and had a hunting cap on his head. He would be riding in a truck at the end of the parade today, directing the entire process.

A reporter named Y. walked up to Tsugami, saying he had been searching for him everywhere. He was worried that the pictures of the parade weren't going to be ready on time, even if the article itself was, and wanted to know if the parade could set out an hour earlier than planned. Tsugami told him to talk to Tashiro and do whatever seemed best.

"The paper is going to be crazy today. The editors are going to hate us," Y. laughed. "Not only do we have two huge lead stories, with the general strike coming up on February 1st and the raid today on Jikōson's compound, we also have to cover this bull parade, and then we've got the special report on 'Traveling with the Bulls.'"

"It'll all be over in a few days," Tsugami said. "Don't pay any attention."

Recently the paper's pages were awash with big news stories, crammed into limited space. All their competitors were paying particularly close attention to what was happening with the strike, and their editors remained resolutely focused on that one issue; Tsugami, meanwhile, kept right on giving most coverage to the bullfight, come what may, telling himself what he had told Y.—pay no attention.

Y. glanced at his watch. "Seven already! Today is one

busy day." He lit a cigarette, expelled a puff of white breath and smoke, and hurried off in Tashiro's direction.

In the end, the parade did get under way earlier than planned: the twenty-two bulls ambled out of the yard at regular intervals, banners dyed with their names hoisted up in front of each one, a handler on each side. Already an eager crowd had collected on the street outside the fence, forming a human wall. As Tsugami stood watching the bulls plod out, Tashiro, who had already climbed into the final truck with the bulls' owners and people from the paper, with their microphones and company flags, made a great show of leaping from the cabin just as it was about to start moving, and came running over to Tsugami.

He had almost forgotten something important, he said, smiling. "Can you get hold of a hundred thousand yen by tomorrow? We'll be okay as long as you have it by two or so." He spoke as though this were nothing at all. "We were supposed to pay the handlers after the tournament, but they say they want it up front. Sorry to trouble you, but that's how it is."

Tsugami felt a sinking sensation. He found it hard to admit that, with this big event coming up the day after tomorrow, the paper didn't have that much money on hand. Tsugami was still groping for a reply when Tashiro spoke again, ever so nonchalantly.

"Let's see... I don't believe there is anything else..." He frowned pensively for a moment, then suddenly raised his hand. "Well, see you around!"

A moment later, he had turned his back to Tsugami and was scampering off toward the truck, his heavyset body tilting forward, the muffler hanging out of his coat, jerking in the wind.

Tsugami returned alone to the paper's office in Osaka. As he was walking up the stairs, a reporter on the night shift who was heading downstairs told him a man had been waiting to see him for two hours and took a business card from his pocket. Looking down at it, Tsugami saw that it belonged to Miura Yoshinosuke, president of Tōyō Pharmaceuticals—a brand-new player in the industry that had been generating enormous sales thanks to a series of ads for a breath freshener called Clean & Cool that had been appearing not only in newspapers and magazines, but in trains, buses, and even on the streets. Tsugami had no reason to know Miura personally, of course, but his flamboyant strategy of plastering every space with ads had occasionally come up in conversation at the Reporters' Club.

"The chief said he didn't know when you'd be back, but the man insisted on waiting. Said he would stay until noon."

When Tsugami stepped into the reception room, Miura was sitting alone with *Time* or some other foreign magazine spread on his lap, marking the text with a red pencil. He immediately sprang to his feet and said crisply, "Hi, my name's Miura."

He was a young man, probably in his late twenties or early thirties, with long sideburns and a red necktie in a large, loose knot; he had the affected air of someone in the film world—an assistant director, perhaps—but he exhibited a certain drive as he rose, an unmistakable energy, like that of a sportsman meeting an opponent.

"Actually, I've got a favor to ask of you. How would you feel about letting my company buy all the tickets for this bullfighting tournament of yours at a twenty percent discount."

Miura lost no time in getting to business; he didn't even seem inclined to sit down. Tsugami felt slightly taken aback, unable to gauge the intentions of a man who had popped up like this without any warning. He gestured for Miura to have a seat, then hastily made an inspection of his elegant attire, from his impeccably white collar to the tips of his well-polished shoes, everything absolutely the best that could be had these days, betraying an overweening desire to make money speak. Next Tsugami shifted his gaze to Miura's face, which was characterized above all by the rather over-intense ambition that burned in his eyes. He had the confidently cheerful, obliging look found among people who have been raised in good families, but at the same time there was a fearlessness in his gaze that could not be attributed entirely to his youth.

When Tsugami did not immediately reply, Miura leisurely took a cigarette case from his pocket, as if to say that he was happy to give Tsugami a moment to think. He extracted an expensive cigarette, lit it, and began slowly blowing out streams of purplish smoke.

"No doubt this sounds like an extremely good deal for us," he said after a time, his tone softer than before, "but in exchange for the twenty percent in sales you would be sacrificing, if you'll forgive me for putting it that way, we would be able to pay you the full cost of the tickets up front, immediately. That means you would be guaranteed not to lose money on this thing, no matter what, even if it rains, even if there's an earthquake."

Miura crossed his legs and gazed at Tsugami, waiting

to see how he would respond. When Tsugami continued to sit there listlessly, saying nothing, Miura added, "Naturally, when I say we would buy all the tickets, this would all happen behind the scenes. As far as the public knows, the paper will still be selling the tickets. That would suit us just fine."

At last, Tsugami spoke. "You buy the tickets at a twenty percent discount, and then what?"

"We advertise."

"Ah."

Tsugami felt his cheek muscles stiffen oddly. Miura's brash confidence, and the way he seemed to be pushing for an immediate answer, stirred up a powerful urge to fight back.

"It would help if you could describe the sort of advertising you plan to do. Then, perhaps, I can consider your proposal."

Tsugami noticed that his tone was as clipped and businesslike as Miura's, and the realization made him slightly annoyed. Miura explained that he wanted to include a small packet of Clean & Cool with each ticket when it was sold. In other words, everyone who attended the bullfight would go away with a packet of Clean & Cool as a giveaway. Ordinarily the packet would be sold for seven yen, so they would be getting a seven-yen prize in addition to getting to see the bullfight. In that sense, it would actually be helping the paper.

"You buy all the tickets at a twenty percent discount and pair each one with a seven-yen giveaway. And do you come out in the red, or in the black?"

"More or less even, I'd say. Either way, it wouldn't be much."

"Meaning," Tsugami said, looking directly at Miura with a slightly sarcastic grin hovering around his mouth, "that you would be able to advertise Clean & Cool for free."

"Precisely. Assuming, that is, that we sell every last ticket, that is. But if we don't—" Now it was Miura's turn to grin. "I lose the cost of whatever we can't sell. It's a sort of gamble, you might say."

Miura looked straight ahead the whole time he was speaking, his manner proud; the only time he lowered his head was when he was lighting a cigarette. Tsugami had no idea whether Miura's proposal truly was a good deal for the paper or not. If the tournament was a success, they would see twenty percent of their total sales of three million three hundred thousand yen—a cool six hundred and sixty thousand yen—go up in a puff of smoke. The thought rankled, it was true, but he couldn't deny the great attraction of having eighty percent of their earnings guaranteed, especially now that Tashiro had asked him to produce one hundred thousand yen and he had no idea how he would get that money. Tsugami's mind was made up, though, when Miura said it was "a sort of gamble," offering the words like a challenge.

"It's generous of you to make the offer, but I'm afraid can't accept it. If packets of Clean & Cool were distributed with every ticket, people might get the impression that your company had put up the capital to sponsor the bullfight."

"I see."

He might have been imagining it, but Tsugami had the sense that for the briefest instant the blood had drained from Miura's face. And so, feeling sure of himself for the first time in the presence of this man so much younger than himself, he tossed out a life preserver. "How about this. I can't let you have all the tickets, but if you really want to be involved, I'll agree to sell you five thousand of the fifty-yen ringside tickets."

"Ringside? No, that won't do." Picking up on the change in Tsugami's mood, perhaps, Miura spoke with the haughtiness of a man refusing a proposal, even though he was the one who had been refused. “Spectators in the special ringside seats are irrelevant in terms of advertising. Even if you were to let us have all the tickets, we wouldn’t be expecting to get anything out of them.”

As Miura saw it, times had changed utterly since the war ended. The old middle class, which had always loved unnecessary little medicines and so on, like Clean & Cool, had been totally wiped out—they would be in the third-tier seats now. The ringside seats would be occupied by members of the new salaried class who couldn’t care less about such products.

“How does this sound?” Miura said. “If you’re going to sell us some tickets anyway, why not let us have all the third-tier seats?”

“No, that won’t work for us. The third-tier tickets will sell no matter what. If anything is going to be left over, it’s the ringside seats. Those are the ones that worry me.”

“Well then, I guess there’s nothing to be done. It’s really too bad, but…” Miura sat sunk in thought for a few seconds; then, resigned, stood up. He turned to face Tsugami directly. “The meteorologists say they expect it to rain the next few days, but I don’t suppose—”

“I’m well aware of that. This was always a gamble for the paper.”

"I see."

Miura reached for his hat, smiling mildly as if to acknowledge that the bargaining was finally done. Tsugami marveled at how skilled he was, this young man, in business matters. As he left, Miura said once again, in a tone without the slightest trace of servility, "Would you mind if I come by once again tomorrow morning at nine, in the hope that you will have reconsidered?"

"By all means. I doubt I'll have changed my mind, though."

Tsugami's tone, too, had become formal. When someone put a knife to Tsugami's neck, it was in his nature to press his own blade to his antagonist's, to keep pressing it in, watching the sharp edge; then, after the agitation of the moment faded, he would look back in disbelief at what he had done. This time was no different. After he saw Miura out, his heart grew heavy and dark, burdened with an inexplicable sadness and exhaustion, and a subtle sense of regret. Given the position he was in right now, no doubt the appropriate thing would have been to negotiate an agreement that turned half the tickets into sure cash, even if he wasn't going to let Miura have all of them. What was it about Miura, he wondered, that had made him refuse to compromise?

But soon the vague discomfort the man had inspired in him faded. Mountains of work awaited him.

Tsugami grabbed a quick lunch near the office, and then, around one o'clock, just when the proofs were coming off the presses, he stopped by the editorial department. Both the articles and the photos dealing with the parade had made it in with no problem; they occupied about a third of the paper. A photo of the parade's departure from Sannomiya Station looked a bit too imposing where it was placed, but with the tournament only two days away it was impossible to be too flashy. The article the young city news reporter had written about the parade had more substance than Tsugami had expected, and a fittingly jokey, sensationalistic tone—it would do. Things were going as well as could be expected, he thought, lighting up a cigarette with a sense of relief, only to remember that he still had to find a hundred thousand yen and arrange for the bulls to get their feed, both before the day was over.

At three, Tashiro left the office and took a car to Okabe Yata's company in Amagasaki. Hanshin Manufacturing was housed in a two-story wooden structure in a corner of a burned-out expanse of land slightly off the highway, up toward the mountains; it was much bigger than he had anticipated. The whole building was painted light blue, and it had an unusual number of windows, each one fitted with a large pane of glass—it had a cheerful atmosphere, reminiscent of a sanitarium. The president's office was a luxuriously spacious room at the end of a hall on the first floor; Okabe was there, slumped in a revolving chair with his arms and legs dangling. He was facing his big, completely bare desk, but as soon as he saw Tsugami he swiveled around, shouting out a welcome, "So you came!" A coal stove was burning in one corner; the heat had made the room stuffy. The sky was overcast, but the entire southern wall was a single huge window, and the light that streamed in through the vast pane left the room almost utterly devoid of shadow, open and bright. Seeing him in this context, Tsugami found that Okabe looked considerably older than he had late last year in that dim basement in the building on Umeda Shinmichi.

He was as genial as ever. Within moments, he'd had an office worker bring whiskey.

"Better than tea, right?" he said. "Today you ought to take it easy."

He kept pressing whiskey on Tsugami, cajoling him to drink two or three glasses while he himself tossed down five or six in his usual rough manner, as if it were medicine rather than alcohol. Once he had a bit to drink, he became noticeably more loquacious. When Tsugami said he couldn't stay too long because the bullfighting tournament was the day after tomorrow, Okabe laughed blithely.

"Listen, you gotta let the underlings do the work. Your job is to come up with the ideas, then have people make it happen. That's all there is to it. Never take on any more responsibility than that. Just look at me. All day I've been here like this, doing nothing. That's how it should be. Of course, that's not to say I'm not needed here. Without me, this company would collapse this very day."

"I'm afraid it's different with newspapers—"

"That's where you're wrong. At any rate, if you're having to run around like this now, it means the bullfight is already a failure. Right? What you gotta do is just forget it all, you can't be bothered. Stay here drinking whiskey with me."

Okabe seemed constantly to be looking back on the path he had taken, delivering lectures on the articles of faith he had invented for himself and abided by, enraptured by the sound of his own voice.

"All right, then. I'll join you," Tsugami said, playing along even though he truly did not have the time for this. "But first, we need to take care of the matter I came to—"

"What matter? I'm all ears."

"I have an urgent need for three hundred and sixty liters each of rice, barley, and sake."

The quantities Tsugami named were much larger than was necessary. He was using this request as a way to plumb the depths of Okabe's personality, his badness or his goodness—to take the measure of this man who, though this was only their second meeting, he had already discovered was peculiarly difficult to figure out. Tsugami was curious to see how Okabe would respond. He explained what the various goods were for, and that he hoped Okabe might be able to deliver them all to the Bullfighting Tournament Office at Hanshin Stadium by noon tomorrow.

"Quite a troublesome guest!" Okabe laughed. Then, "Sure, I can do it."

"And the cost…?"

"Hanshin Manufacturing will donate it all. In celebration of the tournament."

Tsugami protested and asked him to name his price, but Okabe simply chuckled. "This company of mine doesn't need to gobble up a newspaper to get fat. Well, that takes care of business! Now let's drink. I don't know what it is, but I've taken a liking to you, Mr. Tsugami."

Tsugami gave in and took up his glass. He knew he was being tricked, and yet somehow he simply couldn't imagine this small man, happily tossing back glass after glass of whiskey, doing something as grasping and underhanded as loading up a train with goods for the black market without even asking permission.

Okabe called a woman on his staff and had her bring cheese, then told her to prepare something for dinner, too, and bring it in when it was ready. The two men talked and drank for another two hours after that, although in actuality Okabe did almost all the talking, while Tsugami half listened and half mused about the bullfight. Okabe talked about business, and when he was done with that he moved on to politics, then on to religion, women, and so on, his garrulousness finding outlets anywhere and everywhere, moving in all directions. His best observations and critiques seemed to glitter with an odd vibrancy only as long as he was offering them, in his own words; when Tsugami reflected on what he had heard, much of it was reduced to the status of distasteful commonplaces.

At a certain point, as Okabe's speech grew considerably slurred, Tsugami's reporterly habits kicked in and he changed the topic. "Three hundred and sixty liters is a pretty big quantity of rice and barley. How will you get your hands on so much?" All along he had been waiting for an opportunity to ask.

"Oh, there's all kinds of ways," Okabe said, his expression arrogantly disengaged. "Makes sense if you think about it. We send agricultural tools out to farming villages, right? So I have them send up big straw bags. How do you think it looks when you dump two liters of rice into a really big bag? Like nothing, just a little layer at the bottom. Even if someone checked, they'd think it was left over from when the bag was emptied. Ten bags and you get twenty liters. And with a hundred, a thousand..."

Tsugami was feeling sluggish now and his eyelids were growing heavy, both from the accumulated exhaustion of the past few days and because the alcohol was starting to take effect. Glancing over at the windows he realized that it was dark out now; the heat of the room had produced condensation that was running down the glass in innumerable rivulets.

"Say I do business with thirty villages in each prefecture, that's one hundred eighty villages in the six prefectures in the Kinki region alone, and say each of them sends up a hundred bags..."

Okabe must have been drunk, too, judging from the way the hand holding his tumbler was weaving in the air. Tsugami listened to Okabe's calculations, his consciousness a blend of haziness and clarity, unable to decide whether they were legitimate or fake, or to judge whether Okabe himself was a big-time criminal or a petty thief.

*

Tsugami awoke at eight the following morning in the night-duty room at the office. After a simple breakfast in the basement cafeteria, he went up to the editing department on the second floor for the nine-o'clock appointment he had made with Miura. Omoto, who ordinarily only came to the office in the afternoon, was sitting beside the large ceramic hibachi by the window, chatting with three young employees who had been on night duty.

Seeing Tsugami, he called out, "Pretty cloudy. I sure hope it doesn't rain."

The air was bitingly cold now that winter had begun in earnest, but for the past few days the sky had been beautifully clear; according to the radio, though, the run of good weather had started to take a turn for the worse the day before. The temperature had risen suddenly, too, and the sun felt warmer. Both these changes seemed cause for concern.

"I'm sure it will be fine—this weather should last another four or five days," Tsugami said. "And the meteorologists say there's a low pressure system in the south that's heading up east, too."

He had telephoned the observatory the second he got up. From his perspective, though, the more pressing problem was the hundred thousand yen he needed to get to Tashiro by two o'clock. Late the previous night, when he returned from Hanshin Manufacturing, he had called two businessmen he'd had in mind, enduring the throbbing in his head, only to learn that one of the two was unfortunately not at home, having gone up to Tokyo, while the other could probably get the funds together somehow in three or four days, but not in one or two. As emphatically as he had rejected Miura Yoshinosuke's proposal the day before, Tsugami had been recalling the man's face in little flashes ever since he woke up. At this point there just didn't seem to be anywhere else he could go for a hundred thousand yen, despite his big talk; it was Miura's plan or nothing. He mentioned the proposal to Omoto, to see what he would say, and Omoto suddenly turned grave.

"With the sky looking this ominous, my guess is Miura will retract the offer. You should have taken him up on it yesterday." Omoto was clearly displeased with how Tsugami had responded.

"No, I think he'll come," Tsugami said. "He said he would be here at nine, and I don't think he's the sort to back down—he'll keep his word. He's not a man who changes his plans overnight."

In fact, Tsugami suspected Miura would come even if it started raining.

"You're talking about one of the best-known businessmen around," Omoto said sourly.

Tsugami's prediction turned out to be correct, though: Miura turned up five minutes before nine. Soon Tsugami, Omoto, and Miura were sitting around the table in the reception room.

"I'd say there's an eighty percent chance it will rain, twenty percent chance it won't. It's a dangerous tightrope to cross, but I'm ready to put my money on that twenty percent. How about it, Mr. Tsugami? The idea we discussed yesterday..."

Despite the dangerous tightrope metaphor, there was no trace of uncertainty in his attitude. He held his head up in the same proud manner as the day before, keeping a close and equal watch on Omoto and Tsugami, waiting with such unruffled calm for a yes or no that it was almost cheeky. And then something odd happened.

"It's kind of you, but I'm afraid we still can't accept." Omoto, not Tsugami, had spoken. He was coughing so hard that he could hardly breathe. Miura's peculiar assertiveness had gotten on Omoto's nerves in an odd way, and he had started feeling all of a sudden that it would be intolerable to let him make off with six hundred and sixty thousand yen that was practically theirs, as he might well do.

"I see," Miura said, a smile on his lips that could have meant anything at all. He went on to chat for a time about recent economic trends, never once touching on the deal that had been on the table, and then he left, his stride so springy that he looked like a man who had just successfully concluded a negotiation. As soon as he was gone, Omoto and Tsugami returned to the editorial department.

"I'll get the hundred thousand somehow. Let's say I'll have it by noon," Omoto said excitedly. "The weather's going to be fine tomorrow, I'm sure of it. No way we're going to have it rain on us."

After that he went around informing everyone he encountered that it would be nice out tomorrow, as if this were some sort of deeply cherished belief, wiping his nose with his handkerchief practically without pause, and then he hurried off somewhere. Sure enough, he returned slightly past noon with a hundred thousand yen wrapped up in bundles.

As he handed them over to Tsugami, he made sure to add a note of clarification: "I got a friend to lend it to me." His suggestion that it wasn't his own money but a friend's was a sign of his attentiveness to detail—he had factored the interest he would collect into his calculations.

He still had some time until his two o'clock appointment with Tashiro, but Tsugami headed over to the office at the stadium anyway. Tashiro was already waiting when he arrived, warming his crotch over the hibachi, smoking a cigarette. The second he saw Tsugami, he blurted out, "Have you brought what I asked for yesterday?"

Tsugami could see from Tashiro's expression how concerned he was.

"I have. Is this enough?"

Tsugami took the stacks of bills from his briefcase and tossed them loudly on to the table.

"Absolutely! Wonderful, thank you..."

Tashiro picked up the bills and, now moving extraordinarily slowly, started slipping the packets into the big pockets of his leather overcoat. He wrapped those that wouldn't fit in a furoshiki.

"It would have been best for you to have another twenty or thirty thousand available, but I don't like having large sums on cash on me, you know?" Tashiro laughed hoarsely.

Just then a young reporter named M. who had been staying over in the office for the past three or four days came in.

"Mr. Tsugami!" he cried, gesturing exaggeratedly. "I could hardly believe it this morning! Someone comes in at four and shakes me awake, and I go out wondering what's going on and find a truck full of rice and barley and sake!"

When Tsugami had finally left Okabe the previous evening, having refused his insistent invitations to go keep drinking somewhere else, it had been almost nine o'clock. Okabe had finished off a second bottle of whiskey almost entirely by himself, and was noticeably unsteady on his feet, but even so he must have managed, sometime after Tsugami left, to convey to one of his employees in badly slurred speech that he wanted the feed delivered. Tsugami answered M. with a simple "Ah," without shifting his gaze from the stark, cold-looking branches of the trees visible through the window. He seemed to feel Okabe's small, bright eyes looking at him—glinting, no doubt, with a mischievous light.

That night, Tsugami hosted a pre-tournament dinner at a fancy restaurant in Nishinomiya, in part to thank the bulls' owners. A few reporters who had been involved came along, as did Omoto. During the festivities, Tsugami and the others found themselves witnessing a startling scene: the owner of one of the bulls regarded as an obvious contender for first place, a woman named Mitani Hana, suddenly started shouting hysterically, kicked over her tray, and got up from her seat. She was a plump woman whose clothes revealed a certain flair that was hardly typical of a forty-something housewife from a small farm.

"As if I'd drink from a cup *you* filled, Mr. Kawasaki—you of all people! I've put my life on the line for this! Right about now my old man and the kids are dumping cold water over themselves back home, purifying themselves and praying that we win!"

Her expression was pleasantly taut, her face slightly flushed from two or three cups of sake; she leaned unsteadily against one of the sliding, paper-paneled walls as she yelled, her gaze roaming over the faces in the room. She was not drunk. The fierce intensity of her desire to see her bull win had stretched her nerves to the limit, pushing her into a state resembling temporary insanity. The Kawasaki bull stood right up there with the Mitani bull as a potential winner, and when that other bull's owner had filled her cup she had been unable to suppress the gush of antagonism that welled up within her, all the stronger because she was a woman and he was a man.

Tashiro went around the room with his cup, trying to liven the dampened mood. Soon he arrived at Tsugami's place. "Can't blame them," he said. "The owners are bound to get excited with all this attention, being written up so much in the papers and so on."

As Tashiro spoke, it suddenly struck Tsugami that he had entirely forgotten that the bullfight was part of this world. He had forgotten the most essential element of bullfighting. And not only him, but Omoto, Okabe, and Miura, too—they had all lost sight of the simple fact that the bullfight was a fight, a battle between two living creatures. Even Tashiro, who had come to explain Mitani's outburst, was no different…

*

Tsugami awoke in the night-duty room at the office. The second he realized it was raining he jumped out of bed, slid the window open in both directions, and thrust his hands out into the freezing air. Icy raindrops pummeled his bare arms. It didn't seem to have been raining for long. He glanced down at his watch: five o'clock. All at once, as he stood motionless in his pajamas by the window, the dawn cold began penetrating his whole body. He pulled his overcoat on over his pajamas, groped his way down the dark stairs to the editorial department on the second floor, and switched on the lamp on the first desk he came to. He grabbed the phone's receiver, dialed the observatory, and asked the man on the night shift about the day's weather. "Back and forth, clear sometimes, then cloudy," the man said bluntly, his annoyance at having been so rudely woken up evident from his tone. Then he hung up.

Tsugami returned to the night-duty room and went back to bed, but he couldn't sleep. Soon he heard the rain start falling in earnest, with the sound of hail mixed in; every so often it blew in sideways gusts against the window by the bed. At seven he got up. Shortly after, Omoto called.

"Doesn't look good, huh."

"If it's a light rain, we can go ahead. We've still got two hours until nine."

"What are you talking about? It's coming down harder and harder."

Tsugami could picture the annoyance on Omoto's face. At eight, everyone who had been involved in planning the tournament gathered in the office. The rain had been tapering off, then falling harder. They decided to head over to the stadium office as a group to wait and see how things went, loaded themselves into five cars, and left. Raindrops streamed ceaselessly down the car windows as they sped along the Hanshin Highway.

Tashiro was in the office when they arrived, gulping down tea at an incredible pace, his dripping overcoat hung on the peg. "One hell of a mess we've landed in. Well, that's business for you."

The wrinkles on his face stood out today, making him look older than usual; he had an air of calm resignation that seemed like exactly what one would expect of a showman down on his luck. Omoto arrived a few minutes later. It was clear at a glance that he was in a foul mood. He paced restlessly, hardly talking to anyone; from time to time he went out to the stands, then came back all wet, heaved himself down on a chair, and sat slumped in an unpleasantly arrogant manner, stuffing his pipe.

Around ten, the rain turned into a drizzle and the sky brightened.

"It's going to clear up!" someone said.

"Great, we'll start at one," Omoto declared immediately.

"We'll get three thousand people at best. Ah, bull-fighting in the rain!" Tsugami said. He had been quiet all morning; now there was a coldness to his tone that could have been either self-mocking or supercilious, and seemed like a rebuff aimed at everyone around him.

"Two, three thousand is fine!" Omoto said even more firmly. "Rain or snow, anything we can do is better than nothing."

At eleven the sky looked as dreary as ever, but the rain had stopped. The paper's employees went out to every part of town with flyers reading "Bullfight Tournament Today at 2:00" that they posted in stations along the train lines out to the suburbs. They rotated the microphones in the stands, broadcasting an obviously pointless announcement about the two o'clock start toward the largely empty residential areas around the stadium, and toward the stations for the three train lines in the area.

Still, as two o'clock neared, a crowd began to gather. Elderly people, students, children, married women holding bundles wrapped in furoshiki, young men back from the war, young couples in flashy clothes… in short, a perfectly random mix of ticket buyers. From the office window, they could be seen passing in small groups through the plaza outside the stadium.

Tsugami stood on the top level of the infield stands, gazing with a cold and dispassionate eye, as though none of them had anything to do with him, at the crowds of spectators streaming through the dozens of passageways into the vast bowl of the stadium and then scattering in all directions. He checked his watch and calculated that people were pouring into the stands at a rate of about a hundred every ten minutes. The speed seemed to be increasing, but even so they weren't going to have much of an audience by two. The game was over. They had reserved the stadium for as long as it was available, so there was no possibility of extending the tournament even a single day. There could be no rain check. Today, tomorrow, and the day after—they had three days to fight this battle, and that was it. One black spot made it clear almost beyond any doubt how things would turn out.

From where Tsugami stood at the top of the stands,

he could see the paddies and fields stretching all the way to the foot of the Rokkō mountains, and the clumps of factories and small houses that lay strewn across that bleak expanse under a canopy of heavy, dark gray rainclouds. The landscape had a cold, frozen look that made him feel as though he were regarding a landscape painted on a ceramic dish. Close to the peak of Mount Rokkō there were a few white streaks of lingering snow. Those few unmelted patches were the only thing that offered Tsugami any relief from his weariness. It seemed to him that something pure had managed to hold on there, something that had otherwise vanished from this defeated nation, little traces gathering, huddling together, talking quietly among themselves about who knew what. Omoto and five or six of the paper's employees were walking around near the seats that had been prepared for the judges in a corner of the field. Someone had planted the banners dyed with the bulls' names in front of the ringside hitching posts, where they hung limp and heavy, utterly still, as though they had agreed amongst themselves to do this. Not once during all the hectic running around of these past three months had Tsugami imagined the bullfight being like this, so bleak and sad. How enormously different reality was. And yet still he kept everything at arm's length, himself included, turning a detached gaze on all he saw. He didn't even feel the tenacious determination, the urgency that had inspired Omoto to try and find some way, any way to lessen the staggering losses it was already clear the company would suffer. All he felt was an unbearable sense of desolation at the miscalculation he had made, the enormity of which was becoming ever more apparent. He had gripped his opponent as hard as he could, pushing him to the edge of the ring, only to have the tables turned on him at the last second, and find himself being flipped lightly outside. It disgusted him that he had made such a blunder. All morning he had been fighting instinctively against the loss of his self-esteem, his confidence. Never before had his eyes looked so cold and haughty.

In the end, at two o'clock, about five thousand spectators sat spread out around the inside stands. Then, just as Omoto's opening remarks boomed out from the thirty-six speakers mounted throughout the stadium, echoing hollowly through every corner, the rain started again. By the time the first two bulls were led out to the center of the ring, it was falling harder.

T. came over to Tsugami, who was sitting in the judges' area, a look on his face like he just couldn't take it anymore. "Listen, we can't do this. People are starting to leave. Let's call it off."

"I agree," Tsugami said briskly. "Make the announcement." And with that he stood up and strode away, sopping wet, his feet pressing firmly into the earth with each step. He cut diagonally across the field and started climbing the stairs that led into the infield stands. A thousand or so spectators were still standing there, holding umbrellas or with overcoats pulled over their heads, looking fidgety, staring down at the ring, unwilling to give up and go home.

As Tsugami entered the crowd, he began for the first time to despair. No one was sitting on the wet benches, but he did: he lowered himself on to one at the edge of the stands and sat without moving in the pelting rain. When the announcement that the tournament had been suspended came over the loudspeakers, everyone began moving at once, filling the air with the noise of their voices. Tsugami sat stiffly among the heaving masses, struggling desperately to keep something in him from crumbling.

At some point he realized that someone was holding an umbrella over him, protecting him from the rain. Sakiko, he thought immediately, and sure enough, it was her standing beside him.

"Silly, you'll catch cold out here. Come on, get up," she said, her tone commanding. She trained her eyes on him, unmoving, half pitying and half unnerved. Tsugami obediently stood up.

"I think you should just go back to Nishinomiya, don't you?"

Tsugami looked blankly in Sakiko's direction for a moment, his gaze unfocused. Then, coming to himself, he said, "Come wait for me, will you? I've got a few things to take care of."

The next instant he was heading down toward the field, against the crowd. His gait as he descended from one step to the next struck Sakiko as dangerously unsteady. He was totally exhausted. When they reached the field, he led her over to the main exit on the first floor and asked her to wait there while he went alone to the office. By the time he entered the room, he looked like a different man: his face was still pale, but he had regained his usual imposing air. Omoto wasn't there. Tsugami asked after him, and someone said he had taken a car back to the company. Tsugami dried his rain-soaked hair with a handkerchief, combed it, retied his necktie, put a cigarette in his mouth, and then, with a sense of decisiveness so intense it seemed almost abnormal, set about running through one item of business after another with extraordinary speed. He put Tashiro in charge of the bulls and issued orders even more detailed than usual about how the article in the next day's paper should be handled. Finally, in a sort of rebellion against the consideration the paper's employees were showing him, trying to speak as little as possible, he gathered everyone around him and addressed them in a forceful tone that left it unclear whether he was just making an announcement or issuing a command.

"Okay everyone, listen up. If it rains again tomorrow morning, we're canceling the day's fights, even if it clears up in the afternoon. We'll just have to make this thing fly the day after tomorrow!"

About an hour had passed by the time he sent all the remaining employees away and went back out to where Sakiko stood alone and cold at the now deserted exit. They got into the only car still left. Once they were inside, Tsugami leaned back into the seat and closed his eyes. The collar of his wet overcoat had drooped over, covering half his face, and his hat was about to slip off, but he made no move to adjust either. He looked as if he was in terrible pain. Every so often he would bite his lip and groan quietly as he endured it. When Sakiko said something he would nod or shake his head in response, but that was it; he never spoke. She gazed intently at the face of her wounded lover as the taxi rocked him roughly this way and that. For the first time, she saw him—this living being beside her, so badly injured he even couldn't speak—as her own. Like a dissolute son who had gone out and lived it up until everything fell to pieces, leaving him with nowhere else to turn, he had come back to her—yes, to her. An almost maternal sense of victory flickered within her. She felt a strange love for him, paired with a kind of cruel pleasure, and the feeling made her both cold and gentle. She cradled his head in her arms and caressed him freely, as much as she wanted; his expression did not change. Even if she were to withdraw her hands and push him away, his expression would remain the same. Never before in their three years together had she been in a similar position. Until now he had always been pushing her away, pulling her back, then pushing her away again. She wiped his face with her handkerchief, conscious of the driver's eyes. The peculiar, completely unfamiliar desire she felt as she looked down coldly at Tsugami had turned her into a different, much bolder woman.

*

The rain that kept pouring down on the first and second days of the bullfight let up on the evening of the second day. A cold wind was blowing on the third day, but there wasn't a cloud in the sky—it was, so to speak, perfect weather for a bullfight. At nine o'clock they had sold about sixteen thousand tickets, which was far fewer than they had expected but still good.

Omoto stopped by the ticket counter almost every hour, dressed in his morning coat, passionately focused on the question of just how much they would manage to chip away at the enormous losses the paper had sustained. Tashiro, for his part, would periodically climb to the uppermost stands, make a detailed observation of the crowds streaming from the train station to the stadium, and then hurry back down the countless stairs, hampered by the heavy hem of his leather overcoat. All morning he had been mentally running through the same calculations. Unlike Omoto, however, he was subject to intermittent fits of despair. He couldn't sit still. One second he would be in the judges' seating area, the next he would be wandering among the spectators at the edge of the ring, pacing back and forth in front of the hitching posts, and then all of a sudden you would spot him in some remote section of the outfield seats, far from everyone. From time to time he paused, took a small flask of whiskey from his pocket, slowly twisted off the lid, and raised it to his mouth. In any event, neither Omoto nor Tashiro was paying the slightest attention to the central event—the bullfighting. Which bull won and which lost was a matter of no concern: an odd, rather stupid, and indeed senseless competition between two animals, two pairs of locked horns.

Tsugami sat with the judges in the judges' seats, a program and a tall stack of prizes and certificates before him. He might have been imagining it, but he seemed to sense a certain coolness in the gazes of the paper's employees when they looked at him—a combination of sympathy, exultation, and defiance, all aimed at him as the man responsible for the failure of this project. Tsugami had been sitting here since morning, casting his eyes almost randomly at the program, at the ring, and at the spectators who had filled about sixty percent of those rows and rows of benches. The truth, however, was that, like Omoto and Tashiro, he was taking nothing in. He looked at everything and saw nothing: not the matches between the bulls, not the stands or the people, not the scoreboard. The loudspeakers issued an incessant stream of announcements, but his ears heard nothing. As far as he was concerned, this whole absurd, pointless festival was irrelevant. Every so often a fierce northwesterly wind blasted the stadium, causing the decorative curtain behind the judges' seats to whip noisily about and setting the thousands of bits of paper that lay scattered over the field whirling across the ground. Deep in the solitude of his heart he was fixated on a new plan—come summer, he would take the bullfight to Tokyo. He could sell the idea to the Society for the Protection of Cows and Horses, or maybe the Ministry of Agriculture and Forestry, or he could try to get the Ministry of Health and Welfare or the Ministry of Finance interested, persuade them to recognize bullfighting as a form of licensed gambling akin to the lottery. Then he could pay back the huge losses Tashiro had sustained, and somehow compensate the paper for the debt it had incurred. This, he thought, was what he had to do. His failure this time had only dragged him even deeper into that morass—the strange allure of this bullfighting project. The fierce despair that had assaulted him on that rain-drenched first day had smashed like waves on a rock and retreated. The failure of this tournament had left no scar on him at all.

At three o'clock they had sold thirty-one thousand tickets, but it looked as though they had finally reached the limit. They wouldn't be selling many more.

Tashiro came wandering over to the judges' area and sat down on the edge of the table, which was laden with certificates and prizes. "Assuming this is what we've got," he said to Tsugami, "I'd say we're about a million in the red. Even if it's only half that, that's still five hundred thousand. Pretty bad."

One of the judges scolded him for his rudeness, pointing out that people were watching. He called out an apology, slid contritely off the tabletop, and stumbled over to sit beside Tsugami in the seat reserved for the chairman of the event. Giving a hostile sniff that seemed to be aimed at no one in particular, he abruptly plucked the cigarette from Tsugami's lips and used it to light his own. He was quite drunk.

"Five hundred thousand yen isn't much nowadays, Mr. Tsugami, but in my case I borrowed that money from a guy I know, kind of like an older brother to me. High-interest loan. And this guy, he's really not someone you want to mess with. He's a devil, actually, an absolute devil. A stingy, grasping, nasty fiend who doesn't ever give up, that's what he is. Oh, this is awful, just awful!"

Tashiro, clearly in agony, threw his hands into the air and clutched his hair with his fingers for a moment, then buried his head in his arms. Tsugami's eye was drawn to a wide split in the seam of the lining, just inside the cuff of his leather overcoat. Suddenly he found himself wondering for the first time whether Tashiro had a family. He had never mentioned a wife or children; maybe his wife had died or they had split up, and now he was single. Come to think of it, something in his bearing seemed to suggest that he had a sorrowful past.

"Well, Mr. Tsugami, that's business for you. Guess I might as well take another spin around."

Tashiro got to his feet and wandered unsteadily away, hands stuffed deep into his overcoat's big pockets. He weaved through the crowd at the edge of the ring, heading for the hitching posts, walking in a manner that could have been nonchalant or precariously wobbly.

Moments after Tashiro left, Tsugami caught sight of Miura Yoshinosuke striding briskly through the crowd, making a beeline for the judges' seats. The next instant, without even realizing that he was doing it, Tsugami was on his feet. Miura marched on until he was standing just across the table from Tsugami, his eyebrows raised in his usual proud expression but his demeanor otherwise devoid of all emotion. He thanked Tsugami for their meeting the other day, seeming so matter of fact about things that Tsugami thought he would have tried to shake hands if it hadn't been for the table between them.

"I've come today because I'm hoping you might agree to do me a little favor," he began. Neither his words nor his air carried any hint of sarcasm or scornful satisfaction at the miserable end to which the tournament had come, though neither did they carry any suggestion of sympathy or pity. He was here for one reason: to try and strike a bargain. "So how does this sound? I've heard that you have a fireworks display planned for tonight, after the tournament. It would be nice if you would allow me to send up a hundred Clean & Cool coupons with one of the fireworks. Anyone who finds one will be given a package of Clean & Cool as they leave. I'd be happy to cover the cost of the display."

"That will be fine. I'll call the man in charge of the display so you can talk to him. You're welcome to send up a hundred or even two hundred coupons. There's no need to pay for the display. This will be good for us, too—it will brighten the mood."

As soon as they had concluded this exchange, Miura turned toward the field and raised his hand. Two men, evidently employees of his company, ran over. He moved away a short distance and talked with them for a few minutes, then came back over to Tsugami. He was leaving everything to the two men, he said, and would be grateful if Tsugami could ask them to do whatever was necessary. He himself had other business to take care of, so he would be leaving. With that, he hurried off without so much as a glance at the ring.

The whole time he was conversing with Miura, Tsugami had felt a certain tension in his heart. A coldness entered his speech and his attitude, and he found himself stiffening, slipping naturally into a defensive posture. What was it that this man had inside him? What made Tsugami feel such antipathy toward him? Once again, he found himself confronting the same questions that had entered his head at their first meeting. But he remained oblivious. He had not realized that the thing Miura possessed that got his back up had nothing to do with that egoistic refusal to display any emotion, focusing only on the negotiations at hand; nothing to do with his inimitably rational approach, which enabled him to separate business from personal issues with an almost insolent clarity; and nothing to do with that ambitious, arrogant gleam in his eyes—no, it was something altogether different. It was the luck that dogged Miura in everything he did, a sort of destiny that was his birthright, and that stood in perfect contrast to Tsugami's own relentless tendency toward ruin. This was what set them in irreconcilable opposition. Tsugami hated this man who would always defeat him.

Shortly afterward, Tsugami glanced over toward the hitching posts and was surprised to recognize Okabe's diminutive figure among the crowd of spectators. He was walking slowly along with Tashiro in tow, stopping before each bull for a while and then moving on to the next, as if he were assessing them. Okabe and Tashiro were being followed at a slight distance by a small group of men. Tsugami kept losing sight of Okabe as passing spectators blocked his view, then seeing him again, but even so he sensed in the back of that small, suited figure, bathed in the slanting afternoon sunlight, a solidity that was entirely unfamiliar, that he had never before seen in Okabe, as the man made his way calmly, at his leisure, among the crowds. Not all those twenty-two bulls would be returning to W., Tsugami realized. Here he had been foolish enough to think the matter of Okabe's buying the bulls had been settled—all of a sudden, he was struck by the comedy of his own obliviousness. How many bulls would never see W. again? Five? Ten? Or none of them? Tsugami stared at Okabe's small figure as he stood there with his arms folded before a bull, listening placidly as someone told him about the animal, and he felt not rage, exactly, but a sort of self-lacerating satisfaction.

The main attraction of the tournament, the match between the Mitani bull and the Kawasaki bull, had been going on for an hour already and had yet to be decided. The two bulls simply moved from one place to another every so often, from the center of the ring to the edge, then back to the center, their horns locked, the ferocity of their breathing sending ripples across their tremendous frames—it seemed impossible that the balance of power would ever be broken. The match was dull and it had been going on so long that one judge had suggested calling it a draw. In the end Tsugami proposed asking the audience members to show by their applause whether they wanted to let it end in a tie or to let the bulls keep fighting until one of them won. His plan was adopted.

Before long, Mitani Hana, who must have heard the officials discussing the matter, came running over to Tsugami, a hand towel wrapped around her neck. "Please let them keep fighting!" she pleaded. "Even just ten minutes more! You can't let it end in a tie!" Her face was pale from the tension of the long match. "Please, anyone can see which bull is going to win!"

Just then, the loudspeakers announced that the organizers wanted the audience to clap to decide whether the match should be declared a draw, or whether the bulls should keep fighting to the end.

"Those in favor of calling it a tie, let's hear you now!"

Clapping broke out on every side of the field, but surprisingly fewer than a third of the spectators were in favor of ending the match. When the announcer cried out, "And now those in favor of letting them fight!" a much louder wave of applause filled the stadium. The match would continue, as Mitani Hana had hoped.

Tsugami told the judges he was going to take a walk, then left and started climbing into the infield stands behind third base. He had remembered that Sakiko had promised to come this afternoon; she would be sitting in the infield stands, in the top row. In fact, she had been sitting for over an hour in the stands behind first base, near the judges' seats. The bullfighting did not interest her. She found it incomprehensible that Tsugami had put himself through so much for such a boring, slow sport that was also not at all modern, no matter how you looked at it. Her gaze tended to be focused less on the ring than on Tsugami where he sat with the judges. He was no longer the man he had been two days earlier, the man who lay despairing in her arms, as though it were up to her whether he lived or died. His profile, the way moved when he talked with others or issued instructions—everything about him radiated the same restless energy he had always had. Even this far away, she was dazzled by his vibrancy, so typical of a young newspaper director. The day before yesterday, he'd had a place in his heart for her, there was no question of that—an emptiness that only she could fill. Now, thinking back on the certainty she had felt then of his need for her, it seemed oddly tenuous, like a dream. There he was, the same old egoistical Tsugami who could probably have forgotten all about her a year from now, if he wanted to. It was all over now. He would never come back to her. For some reason, this feeling had taken form within her, becoming an unshakable conviction.

Sakiko went up after Tsugami, climbing into the infield stands behind third base. They sat down beside each other on the last bench.

"Nice of you to come. I'm impressed that you remembered me."

This was not irony. He seemed so far away today that such words came naturally.

"That applause just now, when the audience chose to let the Kawasaki and the Mitani bulls fight until one wins—I'd say about seventy percent of this crowd was clapping," Tsugami said suddenly. "Think about that. Seventy percent of the people in this stadium don't find this long, tedious match boring." Until he spoke, his eyes had been roaming around the ring, a look in them that might have been either hostile or disdainful. Now he glanced up and into Sakiko's eyes. "In other words, that's how many people here have placed bets on this competition. It's not which bull wins and which loses that they want to see decided, it's whether they themselves have won or lost."

A faint smile hovered around his mouth. Sakiko thought it looked terribly cold. Sure they're betting, she thought, but didn't your paper make the biggest bet of all? You gambled its whole future on this. Tashiro had placed his bets, too. Omoto had placed his. So had Mitani Hana.

"Yes, everyone is betting. Everyone but you." These words slipped out before Sakiko knew what she was saying.

Tsugami's eyes flashed. They looked proud, but somehow sad.

"It's true. I'm not sure why, but I feel it, seeing you here today." She meant this as an explanation, an attempt to dull the razor-like edge she herself had come to perceive in her earlier comment, but as she spoke a sudden, fierce burst of emotion, half sadness and half anger, came at her out of the blue, making her want to hurl herself bodily against him. When she spoke again, the hatred in her tone was unmistakable. "You've never taken a gamble on anything. You're not a man who ever could."

"And you?" Tsugami had said this casually, but Sakiko caught her breath.

She smiled, the blood draining so completely from her twisted face that even she could feel it. "Yes," she said, cutting each word apart from its neighbors, "I have placed my bets."

It was true—she had. The instant he had asked her that question, she had decided, reflexively, to let the struggle between the two bulls that was playing itself out even now in the middle of the ring decide the issue that had been causing her such agony for so long: whether to break up with Tsugami, or to stay with him. If the red bull won, she would leave him.

She looked out across the stadium. In the ring, two bulls, one red and one black, stood as still as clay statuettes. Now that the rain had let up, cold winter sunlight streamed down on the ring and the bamboo enclosure, and on the crowds surrounding them. The handlers slapped the bulls' buttocks and flanks to rile them up. The banners flapped in the wind; as the match continued to stagnate, the speakers kept repeating the same phrases time after time, spewing out scraps of speech that sounded weary and annoyed, almost shrieking. The stands were eerily quiet. There was no laughter, no conversation; the spectators were all staring down at the ring. Sakiko felt something dark and cold and slow, like twilight, filling the stadium, and it hit her in the chest with a feeling of sadness that was almost more than she could bear.

And then it was over. The quiet shattered as the whole stadium leaped to its feet, cheering. Down in the ring, the balance between the two bulls had finally crumbled, and the raging, pumped-up winner was running around and around the ring, unable to contain the excitement of his victory. Sakiko could not tell at first which of the bulls had won. She felt terribly dizzy. Restraining the urge to reach out and grab Tsugami's shoulder, she kept her eyes on the ring. All she could see was the strange circling of that sorry red beast, stirring and stirring with its bulk the muck of helpless sorrows filling the vast horseshoe of the stadium.

AFTERWORD

I began my career as a novelist in 1949, the year I published *The Hunting Gun*. My next work, *Bullfight*, earned me the Akutagawa Prize, and with that I became a true writer. When I reread these two texts now, whatever qualities and defects they may have as literature, I find myself dazzled by the beginner's enthusiasm that animated me in those days.

I was forty-two when *The Hunting Gun* and *Bullfight* were published. In the span of a man's life this is already verging on old age, but within the context of my life as a writer there is no question that this was my adolescence, and these the works of a very green novelist.

They say that, as authors mature, they follow the trajectory charted by their first writings—a rule to which, it seems, there are no exceptions. If this is correct, then *The Hunting Gun* and *Bullfight* carry within them, alongside their youthful ungainliness, something fundamental from which I have never been able to break free. For this reason, I believe I am more fully present in their pages than in any of my other texts.

Forty years have flowed by since then without my seeing them go, fifty novels of varying length, a hundred and eighty novellas... When I consider the work I have done, I feel a little like I am gazing out at a garden gone to seed. Amaryllises poking up in random places, roses whose appearance leaves much to be desired. The flowers blooming there belong to the most diverse species, large and small, transplanted from the desert and the Himalayas. Weeds are encroaching everywhere. Yes, it is an untended garden. Each time I look upon this landscape, it seems somewhat different. Sometimes, when the sun is shining, I find it filled with clarity. Other days it is sunk in shadow, hushed and gloomy. No matter how it appears to me, though, this untamed garden is me. No one else but me, all there is to me.

Just as men are born under lucky or unlucky stars, so, too, literary works are more or less blessed by fortune. Some arrive in the world perfectly formed; others are born sickly. Certain works achieve celebrity, while others languish in the shadows, condemned to huddle all their lives in an out-of-the-way corner. Whether or not a work meets with success is to some extent a matter of caprice. Works the author approves of are ignored, and vice versa. The destinies of literary works are as fickle as those of men. Among the works I have published, some have had the good fortune to be much discussed, while others were forgotten almost as soon as they saw the light of day.

An author's attachment to his works is not necessarily proportional to their success. On the contrary, he is overwhelmed by the desire to usher into the world works that he has been unable to complete, that remain unfinished. One notices this, naturally, in collections whose contents he himself has selected. This may well be their principal interest.

Some years ago, I put together a collection containing twenty-three texts: *The Hunting Gun* and *Bullfight*, which launched my career as a writer, and other novellas among the many I had written over the years with which I was particularly pleased. Had critics or readers been in charge of the selection, I have no doubt that the results would have been different.

YASUSHI INOUE
Tokyo, 1988

Originally published as the preface to the 1988 edition of
Bullfight *(*Combat de taureaux*)*
published by Editions Stock

Pushkin Press

Pushkin Press was founded in 1997. Having first rediscovered European classics of the twentieth century, Pushkin now publishes novels, essays, memoirs, children's books, and everything from timeless classics to the urgent and contemporary.

This book is part of the Pushkin Collection of paperbacks, designed to be as satisfying as possible to hold and to enjoy. It is typeset in Monotype Baskerville, based on the transitional English serif typeface designed in the mid-eighteenth century by John Baskerville. It was litho-printed on Munken Premium White Paper and notch-bound by the independently owned printer TJ International in Padstow, Cornwall. The cover, with French flaps, was printed on Colorplan Pristine White paper. The paper and cover board are both acid-free and Forest Stewardship Council (FSC) certified.

Pushkin Press publishes the best writing from around the world—great stories, beautifully produced, to be read and read again.